PAY the PIPER

A novella of utter speculation

By Sarah Connell

Speculation Publications

Print ISBN-13: 979-8-9918553-2-7
Ebook ISBN: 979-8-9918553-3-4
Executive Editor: LCW Allingham
Editor: River Eno
Cover Art: Aleeya Marie Jones
Design and Layout: LCW Allingham
Copyright © 2025 Speculation Publications LLC

Vectors and Art: Vecteezy
Fonts: California, Deutsch Gothic
Published by Speculation Publications
No part of this book was created by AI

For More Information go to www.speculationpub.com

To my family, Trev, Mere and Evie, for all the games, adventures, and memories over the years. And my parents, you've been an inspiration to the bibliophile within me since my Narnia days. No one could have better first readers.

And to Jax, for believing in me even when I can't see the way forward.

Sarah Connell

I

The Piper

The day began with the clack of shutters thrown wide, breaking up the quiet of the night until one by one the villagers stirred.

Summer had come to the town and along with it a feast day such as none before. If anyone chanced to look up as they crossed the central square, they would have seen me leaning within the shadows of the cathedral's belfry. My face painted to match the white and red and blue of my motley surcote and cap full of bells.

Voices rose from the square below as villagers dragged out tables from homes and taverns alike until everyone had a place to rest their cup and give their tithe to the newly returned White Bishop. The two guests of honor entered from a manse at the back of the square. I leaned around the edge of a stone pinnacle, shielding my face from the sun. At this height, I could only make out the colors of their robes.

One of black, and the other one of flossy white. They were like two poppies waving in the sun amidst a field of drab browns and greens and faded reds. The Mayor and the Bishop had positioned themselves at the head of the largest table near the steps leading up into the nave. Their heads bowed close until one's tall hat brushed the other's.

Unwashed children and stray dogs ducked between the nervous nobility and grim townspeople brought out of their homes by the feast for the White Bishop. The rabble stole scraps of food and unprotected coin, barely out of reach from the grasping hands of those whose drinks they'd upset or chairs they'd upended. Coughs burst from the silence like the knell of the watch beetle marking death amongst the villagers.

Winter had lingered into an unseasonably cold, wet, spring that left the poorest at the mercy of their neighbors' generosity. None more so than the children left to fend for themselves on the street; those piled into doorways to sleep at night if they were lucky. Others were taken in as orphans of the Church, if caught, to be raised as oblates. It was whispered behind closed doors that the newly returned prelate had a need for all the oblates he could take, purpose unknown.

Few but the oldest among the villagers had lived under the White Bishop's rule. He'd disappeared one night long ago, leaving the town to the discretion of lesser clerics, and the abbott from the nearest monastery a day's walk away. Some said he had been promoted all those years ago and had taken up residence in the more prosperous neighboring territory. But those born and raised in the town who did recognize him gave the warding sign and ducked their heads as he passed. Better to not be seen looking too hard at the figure clad in white who walked with head held high as if he'd never left. And better yet to not be known by him in turn. Those villagers whom he did recognize had a habit of disappearing.

When the sun reached its zenith, the gears of the astronomical clock within the tower clicked. The long hand inched up to cover the short, and the great bell began to toll. I pulled my hat down around my close-shorn flaxen hair, setting the cap's bells to jingling.

Reaching out with hand and foot, I took hold of the bell's rope on the next downstroke. The bellringer pulled far below, and I jumped into the open shaft of dark stone, sliding down. He jumped back as I landed at the bottom in a crouch. The heat from the day hadn't reached the alcove, and yet the man's pallid face dripped with sweat. He looked ill.

"Don't stop now," I called as I took up pulling the rope in the unrelenting rhythm of time. "The whole town will be scratching their heads as to how they lost the hours." I gave the rope two more heaves, letting it dangle me off the ground on the last one for good measure. With a tip of my cap to the stunned bellringer, I strode out into the sunlight heading for the nearest table where the two heads were bent together, white hat touching black.

The smell on the warm wind tested my gag reflex. The mob of children had taken up refuge in the shadows of the western gate leading out of the square, as far from the town guards as they could be. But it wasn't just them I was smelling. The nobles held sachets of herbs to their noses as they spoke, forming a semicircle around the Mayor and the Bishop. And beyond them, I saw the townsfolk up close for the first time. Gaunt, donned in nothing but rags. Their hollow eyes darted from the Bishop to the guards and then down to their meager tithes. Clouds of incense smoke rose from the young clerics as they walked between the rows with the collection baskets, chanting the litanies. Like the children, their faces were wan and pinched with hunger.

I steeled myself and crept along the shadows until I stood close enough to overhear the heated conversation between the two men who were remarkably different even than the nearby nobles. Where the Bishop sat rigid in robes of finest linen, the Mayor's crisp black surcote showed blood red silk beneath the decorative ties, straining against his formidable bulk. The smell of bergamot hair oil radiated from them, cutting through the stench of their people.

"We don't know that there are more rats than normal or that they are for sure the cause of this flux," the White Bishop was saying.

"How else do you explain it?" the Mayor grumbled, wiping the sweat from his upper lip with a red kerchief.

The Bishop gave a flick of his wrist, gold rings glinting in the sunlight. "The poor and the infirm have always been thinned out in late winter. It's the balance of the world."

"This is different." The Mayor leaned even closer, thick lips glistening in the noonday sun so close as to fleck the sparse white hairs sprouting from the Bishop's ear. "Just the other night, my manservant was chased by a horde of the creatures. He had to beat them off with a cudgel!"

The Bishop sighed, eyes fluttering closed. "Exaggerations."

"I'm telling you, they are in *my house*. We should bring the witches back."

His eyes snapped open. "Devil spawn." The Bishop stiffened, lips curling around the words.

They argued as I stepped closer; just another minstrel hired to celebrate the feast.

"Look," the Mayor continued. "I agreed to your campaign against certain troublesome townsfolk. A witch hunt is always good for morale, especially after a hard winter like the one we've had. But that's over now, and anyone can see that the pestilence is tenfold worse than it was just a season ago. We have nary a true healer or herbalist left. Even the cats have disappeared. You have to—"

"*Have* to?" The Bishop's tone was icy. "I think you should remember to whom you address."

The Mayor sat back, the glossy black of his beard twitching beneath his scowl. "And what do you plan to do? Preach to a congregation of the dead? I think you'll find your coffers grow empty as the bodies pile up in the streets and then who will fund your crusade?"

"How dare you—"

"Good morrow." My exaggerated bow made the small bells quiver in my cap.

The pair turned as one when my shadow fell across the table between them.

The Mayor sat back quickly, black cap askew. "Who are you?" he demanded.

"You may call me Piper. I offer you my services."

"Move along, jester." The Mayor turned and waved a hand toward a group of guards already sodden with drink.

"Ah I see." I glanced over. One of the guards swayed toward me, and I stepped around him, leaving him to stumble against the table. "I had thought you were in need of a rat catcher. My mistake."

The Bishop held up a hand to keep the guard at a distance. His peevish eyes shifted to the nearest nobles who were caught up watching a nearby reenactment of the Three Magi. "And how would one such as you help, pray tell?"

"I'm glad you asked." I pulled a thin box from the inner pocket of my surcote, sewn into the fabric for just this purpose. The rowan wood case had been stained black as coal. It gleamed in the sun as I opened it to reveal a flute carved from a single long bone. I placed three fingers gently to the holes, bringing it to my lips in an embrace. And then I began to play.

Song echoed off of the stone buttresses of the cathedral and around the homes and shops lining the square until every head turned in the wake of the soft melody. Some stood and began to draw closer. The children in particular showed their surprise. As one, they stopped squabbling and froze with the hearing of it. Their mouths round with ohs of wonder. The eldest held the youngest in their laps, small fists grabbing onto fingers bouncing up and down with the music.

The melody drifted through the suddenly silent crowd. Soon, another noise could be heard below the playful piping notes. The clicking of claws along cobbled streets grew until it seemed that every dog in the surrounding blocks crowded around the Mayor's long table. They had an orderly way about them not usually seen in strays—no sniffing or barking and only a minimum of tail wagging. Canine eyes glinted at me, heads moving as one with the rhythm of the pipe's highs and lows. Those in front began to circle clockwise around us three, the Mayor and the Bishop stood and backed against the table. The guards watched from their corner of the square, as caught up in shock as the rest.

I drew the instrument away from my lips and grinned at the open-mouthed surprise of the townsfolk until the silence was broken by the dogs who had begun to get restive and soon were off chasing scraps or their own tails or each other.

"What do you say now, Your Grace?" I asked, pleased with my show.

The Bishop had begun to sweat in the heat of midday, his cheeks flushed, and his brow creased. "All I see," he began quietly through lips white with fury, "is a peddler interrupting the faithful with a trick, and not a very good one at that."

My grin broadened as I played my part. "Ever the skeptic, I see."

The Mayor, bolstered by the Bishop's rebuttal, cleared his throat. "We had a traveling circus in town just last week, child. They had a trained bear that would put your dogs here to shame." And with that, he turned back to the guards who, sobered by my trick, hurried forward this time. "I think we've had enough farce for one day."

"Perhaps another demonstration is in order. I should have thought better than to pick such a docile creature as a dog." I pulled the pipe to my lips once more before the armed men could push through the circle of lingering strays sprawled on the cobbles at my feet.

This time, the cheery song of pups was replaced with that of the faintest twitter whispered on the wind. Its melody rose so high and fluttering that the smallest children danced to what the rest could no longer hear.

Within moments, the sky was full of larks, pigeons and doves. All flying down and around to land among the nobles and guards but most of all attracted to the Mayor and Bishop. The more they tried to divest themselves of the creatures, the more the flock followed them, not pecking or grappling, but gently alighting and flying again until the two men looked as if they wore living cloaks of the softest gray-blues.

The rest of the crowd began to murmur. I glanced over to where the children sat, laughing, and one called out, "Where were you all winter? We could've done with a pigeon pie!" That was all the crowd needed, and they burst out into laughter. I smiled around my flute, one step closer to warming their hearts to me.

The song broke apart when the Mayor let out a shout, and the town square was once more cast in a momentary shadow of wings as the birds flew off to roost amongst the rooftops. In the quiet that followed, the villagers watched me uneasily as I bowed within the ring of feathers.

The Bishop, covered in leavings and feathers, stalked off back to the rectory with not so much as a word. The guards along with the young clerics hurried in his wake, trailing intermittent clouds of incense as they hefted the full tithe boxes.

"Behold!" I called. "All beasts obey my song." And then I sketched a final bow, my cap's bells jingling and spoke softly to the Mayor. "You have only to say the word, and your rat problem will be taken care of."

He spat out the soft white of a down feather and eyed the nearby nobles who were pretending not to listen. "Come to my house. We can discuss this there."

"As you wish." My breathing slowed again, my fingers relaxing around my flute.

I surveyed the townspeople as the feast re-commenced with half the revelry as before now that the Bishop's retinue had left. They began to slink away in twos and threes to local taverns, their gaze shifting to where I sat under the shadowed alcove of the nave, a few lingering larks and mangey strays arrayed around me. The nobles too absconded back to their manses, already sniggering behind their jeweled fingers. They would no doubt wait to drink to the Bishop's folly once they were behind the safety of closed doors.

The Mayor, who grumbled to himself as he pushed his large belly up out of the chair, jerked his head at me and crossed the square. The crowd lapsed into silence as he passed. I stood and followed, jingling along in the large man's wake.

Playing to the villagers, I picked up one bangled foot and then the other in an imitation of his rolling stride. Some of the children joined in a line behind me. They imitated my prance while the townsfolk sipped from their cups, eyes darting just to the left or right of me. None dared to watch me dance forward, fear winning out over curiosity. For his part, the Mayor ignored my antics, not stopping even as his household guard held open the front door for him to enter.

The children behind me scattered away when the servant growled at them. I sidestepped him into the dark expanse within. The stone-flagged entryway held the chill of night and felt oddly barren without its central table that had been brought out as the Mayor's tribute to the feast day celebrations. He pushed aside a few spare chairs scattered around the back of the hall and made his way to a large open doorway. Half in shadow and half out, he stopped there, watching me.

"Just this way," he said, taking a lantern from its hook above the doorway and lighting it from a nearby taper.

I turned, feeling the eyes of the half-sober guardsman lingering in the entry. He didn't follow but blocked the daylight to cast the room into even more gloom. I jingled a mock salute before turning my back to him, ears pricked for an ambush. I knew playing my part of a useful minstrel for the Mayor only carried so much weight until our deal had been put to writ.

When I came to the door through which the Mayor had disappeared, I found a damp cellar staircase instead of the meeting hall I'd expected. With careful steps, I subdued the jingling of the small bells at my ankles to descend toward the single lantern—the only source of light cascading up from the cellar.

Rat leavings peppered the corners and crevices of the stone steps where the light touched them. The drying herbs that hung from the ceiling and the acrid smell of lye could do nothing to cut through the overwhelming stench. This level showed all the marks of the infestation. With the Mayor's back turned, I took a moment to look around. Rat nests spilled from nooks along with a cascade of refuse. I craned my neck, catching the glimpse of a human ear, gnawed well and good, within the nearest alcove. I swallowed back bile, meeting the glinting black eyes within.

I pushed aside a blood soaked rag with the tip of my shoe as I poked my head into the nook behind the stairs where the lowest of kitchen servants slept. Fighting back a gag, I loosened the knot of my black neckerchief tied tight to my throat and pulled it up to cover my mouth and nose. The stench was worse here. Ammonia and blood and refuse all mingled with the musk of rats. A prone figure coughed in a far corner, turning away at the light. The rest of the room lay in disarrayed heaps of straw pallets torn apart and filthy. Black and brown shapes scurried among them, fighting and squealing over scraps.

I turned to where he waited for me. "Your servants are kept well, I see."

The Mayor's mouth twisted into a grimace behind his black beard. He took a hooked pole from its place by the door.

This close, I could smell the hot stench of him, sweat and wool and mead. It was not lost on me just how powerful this man was now that we were eye to eye—me on the second to last step, him standing on the downslope of the earthen floor.

He barely had to reach as he placed the lantern on the crook of the pole and set it to hang on a hook above the door.

I breathed a private sigh of relief that he hadn't meant to use the hooked pole on me instead. I skipped the last step to land before him, looking around in mock wonderment to play up my part. Bowls of tightly bound herbs smoked on crockery plinths at the four corners of the low-ceilinged room to help mask the smell. Besides stinging my eyes with their acrid fumes, they did little to nothing for the moldering damp overlayed with the pungent stink of rat urine.

The Mayor turned slowly in the center of the room, hands on hips, disgust etched on his face. "Rats," he spat. "Worse than I've ever seen. And the barracks have it just as bad. Lost more guards than I can count to the flux already. And most of the others have fled. I can't even keep a skeleton crew of servants any longer."

My lips twitched behind my kerchief. "Of course you've tried all the rat catchers, have you? And their dogs?"

The Mayor took a step toward me, eyes shadowed in the lantern light. "We've set bars into the drains, hired dogs, put out poisoned apples. And still, they thrive." He paused, his voice growing with menace. "It's not natural." The trickling of running water could be heard from a low culvert at the back of the room. A set of rudimentary bars had been forced into the stone in an attempt to keep the vermin out.

"I've lived here my whole life. I've watched this town survive plague, famine, every act of God you could imagine. This is something different. If it weren't, you'd be in the stocks for the stunt you pulled out there, and I'd be laughing along with the rest, enjoying my mead." The Mayor took another step forward, and I backed up against the back wall, my foot slipping into the drain. "I know what you are."

"Oh?" I asked, my pulse quickening. "And what is that?"

"A trickster," he breathed, "and a desperate one at that. But scum like you never end up doing what they say and then run off before they can be caught and quartered. Tell me, Piper, do you plan on trying that here?"

"No," I said, tilting my chin. "I never break my word, and I never leave before I get what I'm owed."

The Mayor crossed his arms over his broad chest and took a step back. "Most people won't deal with someone like you. That's why I brought you down here, away from prying ears."

"And away from the White Bishop in particular it would seem," I added, straightening my kerchief that had come askew.

The Mayor grunted. "A man who doesn't admit he is just a man at the end of the day is somewhat less."

I cocked my head, the bells on my hat echoing off the low ceiling. "And here I thought I knew your price already."

"My price?" the Mayor asked. "Don't you mean yours?"

"Yes, yes," I hurried on, returning to the bargain at hand. "As I said, I expect to get what I'm owed. And your...problem," I let my eyes roam across the room to settle at last on his girth, "is a large one."

"Go on, tell me what we'd owe. I can see you're the only one for the job—you and that flute." He eyed the pocket where the case had been secreted away.

"All I ask is what anyone would want."

The Mayor squinted. "Coin?"

"No." I showed my open palms. "Merely a place to call home."

"You want me to give you a house?"

I stifled a sigh. They never seemed to really get it, those who'd never had to fear being singled out as "other" and then punished for it. "A promissory note will suffice, one declaring me and my kin true citizens of this town, always welcome within its walls."

The Mayor seemed to think about this. "Just a note, you say, so the guards won't kick you out for being a vagrant? And you want nothing from the Bishop?" he countered, as if he'd come upon the crux. "He'll not treat with the likes of you."

"My business with him is separate."

That seemed to satisfy him. "Then we have a deal," he said.

"Let's put writ to it, Mayor." I pulled out my flute. His eyebrows rose as I opened the case and withdrew a small needle from the lining. I proffered it to him. "A drop of your blood here." I gestured to the lips of the face carved into the bone mouthpiece of my flute. "Only then will I consider our deal made."

"I'll play your game, Piper. But if so much as one rat remains or you try to swindle me, I'll have that flute of yours broken in half, followed by each of your fingers. Move against me, and you'll never play a song again."

I nodded, acknowledging that this man was not averse to the grotesqueries of strength and power. He'd most certainly used them before with great effect. He hesitated for a moment before waving my needle away. Instead, he pulled a dagger from his belt, pricking his thumb and smearing a drop along the bone lips.

"And so our deal is sealed," I whispered. A shiver ran along the thick hairs of the Mayor's arms at the sudden chill in the room.

II

Lucie

"Lucie!"

The shout echoed around the chicken yard. The squawks and flurry of feathers muffled my curses as I hopped down from the coop roof.

"Coming, Tilo!" I yelled back and danced among the flock, careful not to break any of the precious eggs I was collecting. I bent and grabbed for one that rolled from my discarded basket near the gate.

My older brother appeared around the corner, face screwed up with that look he got. His sandy blond hair plastered to his sweaty forehead above eyes the color of dark honey. The smell of cows and hay lingered about him as he wiped his hands together, brushing off the chaff. He eyed my reed flute from where it poked out of my apron.

"Playing to the birds again, I see."

"They like it." I busied myself with the eggs. Looking caught up in work was the only way to avoid starting an argument. "And even you've said they lay better when I play."

He bent to gather the last few eggs. "You're too old for this nonsense, Lucie," he said. "When I was younger than you are now, I had to take care of the whole farm and make sure you didn't wander into the hearthfire or fall into the water trough."

I sighed at the same old story. "I know. I'm just more work for you. Better that Mama had never asked you to take care of me before she died."

"Don't talk nonsense." He cuffed me, but not too unkindly. "I'm just saying it's about time to do something more than play all day. Have you thought about the abbottess's offer to join the convent as a lay-sister? They've need of musicians."

"Only to chant the litanies," I scoffed and ducked out of his reach. "Why are you trying to get rid of me, Tilo?"

His eyes narrowed, and he looked away. "I'm just trying to protect you. There's those in the village that would have you married and minding a house of your own now that you're older."

I bristled. "You know that's not for me."

"I know," he hurried on. "But you'd at least be safe with the sisters. The abbottess practically runs the neighboring town."

"And how would I know anything about that life? You won't even let me outside our village."

His brows knit together.

I rushed on before he could argue. "Mama used to play the flute too, and she wasn't a nun. I wasn't too young to remember that you used to sing along."

"And she's been gone for almost your whole life now," he murmured. His face fell, and he ran a hand through his hair as if to shake off the memory.

"Come on, sing with me, just this once," I wheedled. "I promise it'll make you feel better. It always does for me."

"Perhaps later." Tilo turned away, his hands clenching into fists before relaxing again. "I heard talk of a trove of gooseberries in the southern forest. I want to get there before some pig herder tramples them all. Don't forget to bank the hearthfire so the bread doesn't burn while I'm gone."

"I could come with you," I offered, not daring to meet his eyes.

"No," he said, quickly. And then, as if he regretted the harshness of his answer, he went on. "You still have your chores to do. I'll be back before dark."

I hesitated before picking up the basketful of eggs, balancing it on my hip. Tilo took up his cap and walking stick, heading off down the lane that wound through the lower pasture and into the forest beyond.

Only recently had Tilo ventured into the greenwood on the outskirts of our farm, and his visits had been increasing of late. Sometimes he came out hours later, covered in scratches. From brambles? I couldn't say. But he never returned with any of the things he'd promised.

Not long ago, he had avoided the woods as much as possible, as all the villagers did. Modern edicts against old superstitions had kept the mysteries of the ancient forest hidden. Yet many still believed in the powers lingering there, and in the movements of the stars above. Those who practiced the old ways did so quietly, on dark cold nights when no one was about to see them. Even as the villagers crossed themselves on the way to church, they'd be sure to set out milk and honey for the hungry spirits on a little stone altar as they passed the path leading within the wood. I'd never felt the pull of the forest gods. Their promises were empty in the keening silence of my mother's absent music.

I did the chores as quickly as I could in the hopes that he'd keep his promise of *perhaps we'll sing later*. I brought in our small herd of stubborn cows and got them set up with fresh tree hay; then, churned the rest of the cream into butter and stored it in the cold cellar for the coming day; finally, I fed the chickens on scraps and bits of weeds from the garden.

A raven called to me from the ancient rowan tree with branches as thick as any other trunk. I looked up and realized it was dusk. Dread that had been creeping in all day surged into panic. Tilo had never been gone for this long. Unbidden, the sickening memory swept through me of being six years old and watching my mother bustle us out of our house, panic etched on her face as she told my brother to take me out of town, to the old farm our father had once tended. She made him promise to take care of me, no matter what. And then I never saw her again. Her parting gift of a kiss made in haste in the guttering candlelight of our open back doorway still felt soft upon my cheek.

I swayed. I couldn't let Tilo disappear into the night too. I took up my hat and stick by the door and ventured forth into the woods.

My hope was that I would meet my brother along the path coming back home, and we could keep each other company in the creeping shadows that always broke first in the deep woods. I patted my flute for comfort but knew better than to take it out to play. The trees had ears, always listening and jealous of their solitude.

At each fork, I took the least-used one. Those were the paths that Tilo must have taken, the only ones leading into the deeper southern groves, overgrown as they were. Even the villagers didn't venture through here to hunt the harts and aurochs that lived within.

Moonlight shone through the branches as I stepped between the roots, going as quickly as I dared. I made a small sign of thanks that it was a full moon. Hope and fear pushed me on. Images warred within me. A happy scene of my brother jumping out to scare me closely followed by the shock of finding his limp form among the bracken, gored and white with blood loss.

I'd never forgotten the time when a fox had broken into the coop, and I'd found the torn up bodies of the hens the next morning with no sign of their killer except for the trail of blood and eviscerated feathers leading into the hedge. I had heard the noises in the night and had been too afraid to leave my bed or even to wake Tilo. I shuddered and pushed the thought away. That wouldn't happen again. If Tilo needed my help, I'd be there. No more waiting at home.

Leaves rustled behind me, breaking me out of my reverie. I spun around. The path behind lay empty in the moonlight.

"Tilo?" I called out. The woods drank my quavering voice as quickly as it left my lips.

A chill ran up the back of my neck. I raised my walking stick out in front of me and turned. A cloaked form stood blocking the way ahead. Her clothing was dark as a shadow beneath a length of white hair bound in a red ribbon. The moonlight caught the web of wrinkles around eyes that glistened with curiosity.

"You should not be here, girl," she whispered. "The woods are dangerous at night."

"Who are you?" I called out, waving my stick at what seemed to be half-demon, half-old woman. Ravens circled above us, cawing.

She reached out and plucked the stick I had been brandishing from my hands as easily as if I were a child. "Do you know what happens to villagers who stray into our woods?"

I swallowed. Voices began to murmur from the trees around me, and my heartbeat quickened as running footsteps crashed through the undergrowth.

"Aythe, wait," the runner spoke from behind her. "That's my sister!" Tilo broke from the tree cover and came to stand between me and the strange woman. He had a fresh cut on the back of his leg where his hose had been torn, and there were no gooseberries in sight.

Aythe cocked her head. "So this is Lucie," she murmured, eyes narrowing. "Yes, I should have known."

I shivered beneath her gaze.

"Let her go," he panted, catching his breath. "Lucie didn't mean to come here. She was just out looking for me, weren't you?" He turned his head a fraction of the way toward me, not taking his eyes off of Aythe. "And if you hadn't kept me here so long with your oath swearings and full moon rituals, this never would have happened."

"Tilo, we both know there are no such things as coincidences," Aythe said. "And a daughter of the Gathering is never lost. She is always right where she should be."

I looked between Aythe and my brother. "What does she mean, Tilo?"

But it was Aythe who answered. "Hasn't Tilo told you of us, child?"

Tilo bristled, hands turning to fists. "We are doing fine on our own, like I've told you. There's no need—" Aythe cut him off with a look before turning back to me.

She gestured to the murmuring trees around us. "We are known as a Gathering—the ones who are chased from our towns and villages for supposed dark deeds."

"A Gathering...as in a coven?" I breathed, icy fingers trailing up my spine.

"That is what some people would call it," Aythe said. She met Tilo's plaintive stare. "But Holda, your mother, didn't like that name."

"Aythe, she's too young," Tilo said.

"No, my mother wasn't one of you." My mind reeled. "She wasn't a witch."

"Child." Aythe stepped in close, cold anger creasing her brow. "Why do you think they burned her?"

III

The Piper

Talk of my performance found its way into every corner of the wealthy river district—the gossip almost more pervasive than the stench of rot on the wind. The few reputable inns that had made it unscathed through the winter, and the latest round of plague, refused to take in the piper who had showed up the Bishop at the welcoming feast. Lore grew into a thing all its own as the townspeople retired for the night, drunk on rarely-had meat and mead alike. Some said I was a fae, come to take vengeance on them for the latest false witch hunt only months earlier. They said that's why the Bishop had stalked back onto holy ground at the very sight of me. If anyone had dared to ask me if I really could control animals with my flute, I would have asked them in turn if they'd like to hear a song meant just for them? And that was a temptation no one could have resisted. Perhaps it was better, then, that the townspeople proved a superstitious lot.

After a day's fruitless searching, I found myself on the outskirts of town, looking up at an inn with a red raven painted on the placard. "How fitting," I murmured to myself, thinking of the symbol for prophecy amongst the old gods. I pushed open the heavy timber door, hoping the raven foretold good fortune.

The innkeeper eyed me from across the common room as I sidestepped the newly returned tables from the town square. I wondered how they had felt upon hearing the Bishop's mandate that all must attend and bring tithes. The benches were all but empty save for a pair of women, sisters by the looks of them, spinning thread by the hearth, a cobbler repainting half a dozen clogs, and a drunk soldier snoring in a pool of beer at the bar.

"Fine evening, good tavern master," I said in my best *I'm normal* affectation.

She crossed her thick arms in response. "The name's Agathe, not *tavern master*. What do you want?"

I straightened. This innkeeper was a little more forward than most. All the others had merely told me there was no room left, watching me so closely, it felt as if I might ruin their reputation just by standing in their common room. I sighed and said for what felt like the tenth time, "I'd like a room for tonight and perhaps the next if possible."

Her eyes narrowed. "What business do you have here? Didn't you see the sign? This is a red inn."

My brow creased at the unfamiliar term. "I'm sorry?"

"You're the minstrel who met with the Mayor after the feast. You've got more nerve than most to come into a red inn, I'll give you that."

"Ah, so you've heard of me, have you?" My high spirits fell as quickly as they'd risen. A night sleeping cramped in a doorway would go a long way to ruining my already fragile plan. "I wouldn't want you to get on the wrong side of the Bishop. But I think you'll find—"

That brought out a throaty chuckle from her. "Woda!" she called.

"What?" came a voice pure as the ring of hammer on anvil from the back room.

"Come hear this."

A woman somewhat younger but much bigger in arm and curve of hip than the tavern master stepped out, wiping flour from her fingers onto her apron. "What is it? I've still got half the pies to do."

In answer, Agathe pointed to me. "Go on," she said.

"I'm sorry?" I asked, voice higher than usual under the glare of the two women. "I feel like I'm missing something."

"Just tell her what you told me."

"Well," I began, looking from one to the other, "I said I didn't want you to get in trouble with the Bishop for my sake but I—"

This time, the one called Woda burst into a raucous cackle that made the drunk at the bar start up with a snort. "You think someone as scrawny as you could make trouble for a red inn?" she asked.

"Well, why not?" I asked, feeling the heat of equal parts hurt pride and exhaustion begin to simmer. I clamped my jaw to keep from saying something I'd regret.

Woda, still caught up in the joke, waved a floured hand at me before disappearing into the back again.

Agathe snorted. "Wrong side of the Bishop? Minstrel, if it weren't for the Mayor's good graces after his wife passed, she was one of our own, rest her soul," Agathe murmured before continuing, "the Bishop would have had all the red inns burned and the women who run them exiled or locked inside as the pyre took! Plus, as long as we pay our tithes, we seem to be beneath *his worship's* notice." She eyed me as I took this in. "Why would putting you up make the Bishop angry?"

"Oh," I said, belatedly, my mind whirring with the implications of what a red inn really meant. "No, I just..." I swallowed and tried again under her stare. "I'm doing a job for the town, that's all." I scratched my forehead beneath the sweaty band of my cap, trying to think of where I'd heard that name before. "A red inn, you said?"

"Didn't you see the sign above the door?" she asked, pointing.

"The red raven." I nodded, not wanting to give away my hope for a good omen from the old gods.

"Perhaps where you come from, a red tavern sign means something different," Agathe supplied loudly, chuckling to herself. I could feel the soldier at the bar now watching me intently, and my cheeks began to burn.

"And perhaps, where you come from, it's not considered rude to laugh at a guest," I snapped, my temper rising.

Agathe rolled her eyes, unbothered by my outburst. "Since you seem to be a bit daft, I'll say it plainly. This is a *red* inn—as in the blood moon."

I blinked. The fabled blood moon, the cycle where the veil between this world and the spirit world grew thin, when the other world walked side by side with ours. Realization slowly dawned as I looked between the symbols carved above the kitchen door. I recognized them as runes. They were ancient symbols for protection, defense and connection.

"You welcome those of the old beliefs," I whispered.

"Yes," she nodded, speaking slowly as if I was a child. "We are a safe haven, a gathering place for travelers and townspeople alike who hold to the ancient ways."

"But why choose a red raven as your symbol?" I asked. "Why not make it a blood moon?"

"Because the Red Moon Inn was taken."

"As is the Ruby Red Hose!" Woda called from the kitchen.

Agathe winked.

"Oh," I said, smiling now.

"The Ruby Red Hose is actually quite a nice establishment about two bridges north of here. Besides," she added, growing serious once again, "anyone with two wits about them knows a red tavern sign means a red inn."

I glanced over to the soldier who was trying to sluice the spilled beer from the counter back into the tankard as she pretended not to listen to our conversation. I held onto the bar to keep from showing just how exhausted I was. I didn't have it in me to walk another ten steps, much less find another inn to try. I thought about trying my luck sleeping on the rooftops or in a doorway but knew I needed more safety than that. The Bishop would surely have his men out looking for me, hoping for an easy target, and the sun was going down.

"The town used to have a lot more red inns," Agathe was saying. "But once the Bishop got rid of a good bit of the town's more adventurous womenfolk, claiming every last one was a witch, a lot of red inns closed up shop. Used to have a real crowd coming in here." Her eyes drifted around the mostly empty common room.

I took a moment to ponder this, hands gripping the polished wood of the counter in deliberation. I'd never thought such a place as a red inn could have existed. It changed something about the town in my mind, softened it.

I felt every inch of the road I'd walked that day in the soles of my feet. If I didn't find a place to sleep soon, I'd wind up falling asleep on the cobblestones.

I drummed my fingers on the counter, trying for nonchalance. "What if I were to convince you that I'm not like the Bishop?" I said, just loud enough for her to hear. I glanced over at the nearby mercenary who seemed to be contemplating the dregs of her cup.

"There was a time when you could've persuaded me to let an outsider in just by the mere suggestion that it would rankle the White Bishop." Agathe leaned in close. "But we've had some dark days since his coming, and I find I'm in need of a bit more than that."

I took a deep breath. My stomach clenched as I said, "What if I'm not what I seem?"

Agathe's brow furrowed. "What do you mean?"

"We haven't been properly introduced," I said, straightening and trying for a confidence I did not feel. "My name—or at least the one I was born into—is Lucie. I'm a daughter of the Gathering."

Agathe straightened, mouth agape for just a moment before her lips puckered as she looked me up and down. I'd come to dread this part, never wanting to show those outside of my people, who I truly am beneath the mask and revelry of the Piper. When someone learns something they think should change me, it's like watching a fire come alight. I never could tell where it would lead until it was too late. It could smolder into coals, warm and pleasant and home-like or the flames could rage, burning through everything around it until nothing but ash was left.

Agathe's gaze was inscrutable. "In that case, we have only one question to ask here in order for a traveler to gain entry. What's your mother's name?"

I swallowed and straightened. I hadn't spoken her name in so long it felt odd as it passed my tongue, and my voice cracked on the first try. I took a deep breath, steadying my shaking hands, one clasping my flute case deep within my pocket, as I said, "My mother was called Holda."

She watched me for a few heartbeats, and I began to tense, ready to run in case she called Woda back out to hurry me along.

"I see," was all she said.

"That's it?" I stammered, my heart thudding back into its normal rhythm.

"Best get you a room, then." And she was off bustling among the sheets in the linen cupboard.

I swallowed. "No more questions or tests?" I asked, following her up the rickety back stairs.

"None needed," she called over her shoulder and then she stilled. Her voice came rough when she said, "I was about your age when your mother was burned. You belong here."

I felt numb. The mention of my mother and her death washed over me as if a ghost had walked through me where I stood. "You have my thanks," was all I could say as she set the linen on the bed and showed me where to find the wash basin.

"I expect you're here to do a job of some kind and can pay me at the end of the stay?"

I nodded, coming back to myself. "The Mayor has hired me."

"And if he doesn't pay you?" Her voice was pitched high, an attempt at unconcern. But I knew how I looked. Bedraggled and half-awake. I didn't inspire confidence.

"Oh, he gave me his word," I said quickly, thinking back to the droplet of bright red blood hitting my flute. "The deal has been sealed." I felt the Piper within me flare to life at the memory of the blood oath. A smile creased my lips until my cheeks hurt. I was suddenly glad Agathe's back was turned so that she couldn't see me change back into the Piper for that wicked moment.

"Good. For better or for worse, he can't go back on an oath with one of us, now can he?"

I stifled a mischievous giggle and clapped my hand across my mouth.

She bustled out into the hall. "Come down for supper. Woda may look mean when she's about her piemaking, but her pastry is nothing short of pure love in a mouthful."

I could tell Agathe wanted to say something more by the way her gaze fell on my ratty motley and lack of a bag, but she left without another word. I sank to the floor by the room's small attic window, doffing my cap and balling it between my hands. I'd done it. I'd made it to town and gotten the Mayor to agree to my terms.

All that was left was to get to the Bishop, the King Rat himself. Taking up a square of scrap cloth tucked within one of my many hidden pockets, I began to scrape the motley paint from my face. Black streaked through the white on my cheeks, turning from grey to rudy pink until I recognized my reflection in the wash basin once more. I smiled.

IV

Lucie

Mama a witch? The thought made me dizzy.

My ears rang as I whirled to watch the people of the Gathering surround me. Men and women moved amongst the trees until they were a part of the forest itself. Of all ages and creeds, each wore a dark cloak and held a walking staff tipped with a shuttered lantern to cast dim circles of light upon the bracken at their feet.

"It isn't true—is it?" I turned to Tilo, awe as much a part of my voice as accusation. "Was she a witch?"

"We don't call ourselves that," a man said from within the crowd.

"Those are the accusations of the ones who would burn us," Aythe added.

"Then who are you?" I asked.

"We are villagers just like you," one said.

"We're scapegoats," another called from where he leaned against an oak tree. He nodded to me as I turned to him. "Any time there's a tragedy, we're the ones they blame."

"Because you practice dark arts," I whispered, knowing only what the nuns at the song schools taught of witches.

"You use familiars and sacrifices…" My blood ran cold at the word, but I held my head up high.

"Lies." Aythe spit on the ground between my feet, and I shuffled back a step. "There's nothing dark in the rituals we know." The Gathering began to mutter at this.

"Not unless you count refusing to pay tithes!"

"Or speaking out at a trial."

"Or trying to feed your family."

Scorn was written across Aythe's scowl. "Or to try to make a place for yourself in the world."

"Why would that get you exiled?"

"Has your brother never told you of the White Bishop?" she asked. "We call him King Rat."

I shivered.

The crowd jeered.

"King Rat?" I asked, a cold finger of recognition from long ago running down my spine. A remembered shout from the shadows of my childhood…

…the Rat himself is coming! You must hide! Take your sister and go to the farm, quickly!

"She's younger than she looks," Tilo said, stepping forward. "She's not ready for this. It'll only put her in danger."

"All these years," I said, turning to him, "you said it was plague that made us flee the town."

"Lucie, let me handle this." He wouldn't meet my eyes. "We can discuss it all later."

"And you always said it was sickness that had carried her off. Was she really the best healer in town or was that a lie too?"

Tilo looked as if he'd been slapped. "I never lied to you."

Aythe broke in. "It was a kind of sickness that turned the Bishop against a good woman like your mother—one of fear and blame and hatred."

But I only had eyes for Tilo. A fist of cold anger gripped my heart. I wanted to lash out at him, to make him feel what I now felt. "She died because she was a witch?"

Tilo hung his head in resignation, and my anger blossomed, cold and hungry. I breathed deeply, trying to come back to myself. But everything felt wrong. What I'd known about my past, who I'd always thought I'd been, now lay twisted before me. I could feel the strange woman's eyes on me too, and I didn't like it.

"She's tall and slim as a willow switch," someone murmured with a creaking voice from behind me.

"Strong too. Just like Holda at that age," Aythe agreed, her eyes glinting with something other than scorn. "A long time since we've seen her kind."

"Yes, and look what happened to the last that came along," said the old woman from behind me. "Her mother burned up, and these children left to fend for themselves in ignorance."

That broke me. All my carefully preserved collection of memories rose up: the smell of my mother as she mixed herbs and spun thread, the feel of her hair tickling my cheek as she carried me on her hip, and, stronger than all, of her playing the pipe with dancing fingers and smiling eyes in the hearthlight.

"Don't talk about her like that!" I seethed to the old woman, reaching for her. I felt the quick slap of my traveling stick whip out and hit me across the shoulder blades before I could grab at the halo of white hair.

"We do not attack out of anger," Aythe said, her voice cutting through the chatter in the windless night. She held out the stick she'd taken from me before dropping it at my feet. "Might is the way of the powerful, and it corrupts just as surely as any vice. Or did your nuns not teach you that?"

"They tried," Tilo said. He pulled me behind him, and I winced. My back stung where the welt rose along the knobbly part of my neck. "But Lucie's always been stubborn. Aythe, I tell you, she's not ready for this."

My chest tightened. I no longer felt like the child he thought I was.

The glade began to buzz again with the chatter of the men and women. I was reminded of the rustle of dead leaves in autumn when the wind picked up amongst the birch trees. Suddenly, all the tales of the fae folk living in this forest made sense. The twinkling lights that moved amongst the trees as if on their own, and the offerings of milk and honey during feast times that disappeared without a trace.

"I've kept her out of this for all these years," Tilo was saying. "I won't see her caught up in your vengeance."

The knowledge that Tilo had been keeping this secret from me all my life, had chosen to lie to me day in and day out, snuffed my anger and filled my heart with sorrow. Had I ever really known him? And what of myself—how could I say I knew who I was if the biggest part of me had been kept hidden?

I pushed out from behind my brother. "You were as old as I am now when she died," I said, reminding him of his earlier lecture. "If she was..." I swallowed back the bile that rose at the thought, "burned. Then I want to know the truth..

"Why have you kept this from her?" Aythe asked, glaring at Tilo. "I know I've only just arrived back, but I would have thought you'd have done a better job of raising her."

"I kept her alive," he murmured, his eyes pleading with me.

"It is her birthright," Aythe said. "Holda said as much when the girl was born. She was meant to take on the gift."

My brother turned his head away, looking at the ground. "Lucie isn't like us," he finally whispered. "She doesn't remember having to run from everything we'd ever known. She's free from that life."

"Holda was innocent once too, and I tried to do the same for her." Aythe's voice was heavy with loss and something akin to longing. "But all the goodness and lifesong within her came to nothing when she found herself up against the power of the White Bishop. Better to give Lucie her full birthright than to hide it away and hope the future never comes." Aythe's gaze strayed down to the crudely carved reed pipe in my pocket. She smiled. It was a shocking sight—sharp and yellow in the moonlight. "I see she already has a piece of her destiny."

I put a hand to my flute to protect it from these people of the woods.

"Tonight's a good night," the woman on the path behind me murmured and gently brushed the fingers of my right hand as she walked past.

"Yes. It's a full moon," another agreed, and pushed a lock of my hair behind my ear before she went on her way. "So like Holda," I thought I heard her murmur.

Aythe laid a hand on Tilo's shoulder, her face gentling from the keenness it had shown all night. "Tell her tonight. You as her kin should be the one." At Aythe's final words to Tilo, the Gathering walked silently back into the woods, going their separate ways with nothing but the moonlight and the sway of their shuttered lamps like fireflies to guide them. We left too, Tilo taking hold of my wrist to keep me from falling along the rooted path. Not a word passed between us until we reached the lane again that led between our fields.

Back at the house, with a candle between us and a piece of buttered bread each, Tilo stood and reached into a hiding place within the kitchen eave. He pulled out a long box carved from black wood and placed it in my hands. "This flute was our mother's."

My hands shook, and I clenched them beneath the table.

"It is said to have been carved from the rib of an ancient lindworm. The animal's spirit is imbued within. It has the power to control the creatures of forest, lake, and dell."

"Magic," I said in awe.

The hint of a smile creased his lips. "There is a kind of magic in nature, you could say. Some of us can find the tune of it better than others. Our mother was one of those people, and she always thought you were too."

I traced the jagged spine of the lindworm engraved upon the box with a trembling finger. "Why didn't you tell me before about how she died?"

Tilo's hand covered mine, and I met his eyes. "I don't expect you to forgive me for keeping this from you. She'd always meant for you to have it. But I hope you can understand *why* I did it."

"Mama died because of this flute." My voice was small, and my heart felt as if it was being squeezed.

"No." He frowned. "Aythe always said that our mother died because she stood up to a man who thought nothing of killing her for it. I knew if I told you the truth along with giving you the flute that you would have to finish her story. But now I see that was not my choice to make." He squeezed my hand. "This will change you either way. But we can still choose to leave it hidden and go back to our lives."

I gave him a rueful smile. "What, and send me off to sing for the nuns?"

He grimaced. "I think you'll find that becoming part of the Gathering has its own downsides."

"Like Aythe?"

"Yes," Tilo said seriously. "Aythe wants nothing more than for you to take up where our mother left off. She wants you to open it."

My hands clenched around the box. "And what if I want to open it too?" I knew as soon as I said it that I would never be able to let him take it away from me, not after I'd held it in my hands.

"The flute can only show you another side of who you are, for better or for worse."

I looked up at him, thinking back to all the times I'd snuck off to carve finger holes into rough-hewn reed pipes and trying out tunes that warbled like birdsong. I'd felt half-made myself, unable to play the song of my heart.

"Tilo, this is all I've ever wanted," I said.
He crossed his arms and nodded once, eyes brimming as I opened the case.

V

The Piper

I woke with the dawn and was out into the streets before the second cock's crow.

I took small pots of ground lily root and beeswax from an inner pocket to paint my face into the Piper once more. I'd washed my threadbare motley surcote in the washbasin the night before, and it was stiff at the knee and elbow from the time spent drying above the windowsill. The sharp tang of lye soap did little to cover the stale body odor from the prior day's travel. But my sore muscles soon settled into a comfortable rhythm.

The bright light of day showed me what I had missed on my travels here the night before. This section on the outskirts of town looked to have survived the recent pestilence better than the wealthy river district. As I moved closer to the cathedral, most of the shops and homes still had their shutters latched. A few townspeople hurried up the main thoroughfare, picking over baskets of blighted vegetables, scraps of cloth held to their noses in an attempt to blot out the stench of cabbages and potatoes half-rotted from the wet weather. As the sun rose higher and the manses along my route grew larger, piles of refuse crowded every drain of the streets along the quay until the flies became unbearable.

A makeshift pyre had been set up in an open space near the main thoroughfare. Young clerics carried in bundles of wood beneath the watchful eye of the city guard. A promise, it would seem, to any of the exiled witches who thought to return home.

Those with enough coin to purchase what they needed, or what was available, darted glances at the hungry figures leaning in doorways or out of windows. Each group shuttled from stall to stall, a few with a guard or two. All gave me a wide berth.

The crowd parted in front of me, and I came upon a man lying in the road, face down, and covered in his own filth. His mouth was a mask of sores and moved with flies. One hand splayed out, blackened fingers closed around a spilled wine skin leaking into the dirt. He didn't look much older than Tilo.

"Hark now, what's the point of paying my taxes if the Mayor leaves our streets full of bodies each night?" I heard one shopkeeper ask his fellow.

"Is he dead?" another added, peering from a stall across the way.

"Dead drunk," a guard replied, laughing as he kicked him. The man rolled over with a groan into the gutter.

"There, he's out of your way now." The guard said, scowling, as if daring the shopkeeper to make more of an argument.

"Most kind, sir," the merchant said through gritted teeth.

"And thank you for the generosity of more flies around my stall," another mumbled, pulling a kerchief tighter.

My heart pounded, and I found it hard to keep my Piper's bravado in place. I wanted to shrink inside myself, to hide from the callousness of these people. I hurried down a side street into the shade of a nearby alcove to catch my breath before anyone noticed me staring.

A gang of children ran by. One of them held the fallen wineskin aloft as if it were the greatest of prizes. The youngest of the rabble weren't even clothed except for a ragged blanket clutched around them. Covered in dirt and soot, the mark of neglect was written on their half-healed cuts and jerky movements at every noise. A sharp pain sank into my chest, a dagger of memory. These were the lost children of those who hadn't been able to escape and hide in the woods. These were the orphans of the burned. And like Tilo and I, the Bishop had cut them adrift from their families.

"Look! It's that minstrel," one called, pointing, breaking me out of my reverie.

I tried to smile as I bowed, wondering if this was the same group who had watched me in the square yesterday. I tipped my jingling cap to them and they hooted, staring at my freshly painted white face with black diamonds around each eye.

"Play us a song!" they yelled, keeping back, hugging each other in their excitement.

A guard's whistle trilled from the alley's mouth. They whipped around as if they were a herd of feral cats before running off. One limped after, hollow eyes turning to me as they passed.

"Soon, I'll play you a song of safety and home," I murmured, my resolve quickening.

I walked onward toward the smell of baking bread and frothing milk splashing into cowherds' pails amidst fresh straw. I'd reached the rectory at the back of the cathedral grounds.

"Good morrow!" I called to the groom brushing down a bay gelding in the stables. "Is His Excellency within?"

The groom looked at me open mouthed as if I was a walking, talking marionette from one of the traveling puppet shows, and perhaps, I was as close to that as one could get. "No, Minstrel," he said once he'd regained his tongue.

"Piper will do." I tried to put him more at his ease, glad he was speaking to me at all. "Do you know how long he'll be away?"

The groom scratched his head. "Most of the morning."

"Visiting the poor and downtrodden?" I asked, with a glint of a smile.

The groom shook his head, looking confused. He probably wondered if I truly was slow-witted. "His Grace breakfasts at the merchant's guild."

I cocked my head. This lad had nothing of the slow-witted acquiescence I'd come to expect in the townsfolk. He had a spark of kindness about him that made me want to lean in. But I kept my Piper's mask on. "Ah yes. Yesterday was a feast day." The coffers were always fullest after a holy day tithing. It seemed the Bishop was putting Church monies to quick use in wooing the merchant's guild. "Thank you." I quickly doffed my cap and left.

Instead of going in through the rectory to await his return, I headed for the kitchens. As with the Mayor's house, they were near to empty when they should have been bustling with the day's preparations. The door to the sleeping alcove in the side hallway stood ajar, and rats scurried along the edge of the walls. The acrid smell of old bedding and filth cloyed at me, and I turned away. Only a few cooks were at the baking and roasting stations set within the large stone walls. They looked distractedly now and then at the open stairs leading down into the cellar.

Next to the hearth fire, a pallet had been made up for a kitchen servant. Bundled in a blanket with more holes than cloth, he breathed heavily, sores thick on the corners of his mouth. He held a large metal ladle limply in one hand. Bits of blood and black fur stuck to it.

"Hello," I called from the doorway.

One glanced over. "You're that minstrel we've been hearing about?" she scowled. The others turned toward me now, interest piqued.

"Why, yes, I am. I'm on business from the Mayor." I flourished a bow, my heart thudding in my chest under their stares. "I've been tasked with looking into the uh—" I hesitated, not wanting to say pestilence, "the cellars," I finished instead.

The cook who had spoken first gave me a knowing look. "We've got no problems here," she said.

"I'd noticed you seem short on helpers. Is that a recent trouble?" At this the others turned back to their work, ducking their heads almost in unison. The boy by the hearth coughed wetly.

"Have a look, if you must," said the cook. "But I've got work to finish."

With that I sidled forward and began to descend into the poorly lit cellar below. It was the same as the Mayor's house, only bigger. Full of droppings and chewed crates, it reeked of vermin. A shiver rolled through me. A distant patter echoed across the walls, but when I turned to look, it was nothing more than the drain at the end of one wall and the trickle of water on the other side. Blankets were piled into a barrel in one nook with lye and herbs sprinkled along with clumps of straw damp with blood and urine. The barrel had been marked for burning with the red X of plague.

"That would explain the absence of kitchen help here too," I murmured.

The cooks avoided looking at me as I ascended and walked out into the sunlit courtyard. The fresh air felt like a gift.

The groom was still alone with his charge.

"Where is everyone?" I asked.

He looked nervously around him. "I'm not sure what you mean."

"Shouldn't there be other grooms and clergy and such about the place? Is everyone still hungover from the feast?"

This won me a grin. "No, Minstrel...I mean, Piper. Some took sick and others, well, they've left."

"Left the service of the Bishop?"

"No, they left town. Most have joined the pilgrimage."

Pilgrimage or exile? I wanted to ask, thinking back to the witch trials and how others had been run out of town by the Bishop earlier in the year. "Yes," I said instead. "It would make sense to cull the flock closest to home."

"What was that?" the groom asked, tilting his head.

"Nothing, thank you for a piece of your day." I paused. "I'm sorry, what was your name?"

"Adelbert," he supplied easily.

"Adelbert. I won't forget it. Which way to the latrines?" I asked, thinking of where an old man's first stop would be after a heavy breakfast with the merchant's guild. It would be my best chance at getting him alone, no matter how long I had to wait.

He pointed off to a southern-facing building, confusion showing in his eyes, but he asked nothing more.

As I'd hoped, the latrines were spacious, made of stone separated by wooden posts across from a trough that lined the outer wall. I had gotten used to the smell of decay within the town, but the open sewer was by far more potent. I pulled a sprig from a bundle of dried lavender that hung from the rafters and made a sachet from it with my neckerchief to tie against my nose.

Apart from the occasional rat squeak, I was alone. None of the windows had panes so that the warm summer breeze whistled through. I put one foot into a notch in the wall and climbed until I was up amongst the rafters, mostly hidden in the eave above the doorway. The fresh air helped with the stench.

My hands found my flute case to pass the time, and the melody that began to drift about was one I'd been playing since inheriting the instrument—a song of lonesomeness, of un-belonging to anything other than the music and to oneself. It was my song and that of the flute. Lone spiders came out of their nooks to crowd around me as I played. And from the tree branches on the other side of the nearest window, a solitary lark hopped and flew along until it alighted on my shoulder. I wondered at its response to a song that usually called only the most solitary of creatures. I knew if I stopped my tune, it would depart, wild once more. And so I watched it.

The door creaked open, and I broke off, the bird retreating to a windowsill. I tensed for a moment before realizing that indeed my gamble had paid off. The white-robed form of the Bishop hurried in below my dangling feet. He muttered to himself as he removed the finery of his robe and hat, hanging them on a hook before making his way into an alcove farther down wearing nothing more than a white cassock. I glanced out of the slit window into the courtyard where Adelbert stood tending to the carriage horses. A group of guards milled about by the back gate before entering the refectory.

I lowered myself slowly, notch by notch, silencing my bells with each practiced movement. The Bishop was grunting in the farthest stall. I straightened and took a deep breath to steady myself before removing my sachet from my nose. The Piper within me rose up and took hold as I rounded the corner.

"Good morning, Your Grace!"

The Bishop fell onto the open latrine floor, cassock shifting down to cover knobbly knees. "What—What are you doing in here? Guards!"

"No one's out there save for a stablehand." I stood over him, blocking him from getting up. "Don't worry. I'm only here to talk."

He squinted at me. "You're that mad minstrel from yesterday." He scrambled, trying to get up, and I pushed him back down with my foot. He threw his hands back to steady himself and then gasped as the sludge squished up between his fingers.

"I'm pleased you remember me. I'm called Piper." I nodded, letting my cap jangle. "And I came to make you an offer," I said, resting one foot on his chest.

His eyes glinted. "You attack me. And still expect me to treat with you?"

"Oh, I think you'll like my bargain once you hear it. And, you see, you didn't leave me much choice. I knew if I'd shown my face in your antechamber, you'd have me pilloried quicker than I could pull out my flute."

The Bishop only glared at me.

"Let's make this short so we can both be on our way." I stepped back a pace, allowing him to sit up and shake off his hands. His eyes darted to the door and then slowly back to me.

No guards were coming.

"I'm not paying you anything," he said at last. "The infestation is the Mayor's business, not mine."

"Tsk, tsk tsk," I said, wagging a finger. "No need to count your coin so quickly. I already have a deal with the Mayor to rid this town of all its vermin."

He waved a hand and grunted. "I have little time for your madness. Just tell me what you want."

I could feel the cold fist of anger begin to tighten around my insides at his continued derision. I had expected some modicum of fear. But it seemed his privilege and ego remained unshakeable even in the stench of the latrines.

"Your Grace," I said, letting my voice drip with mockery, "you could not begin to fathom what I *want*. But, let's start with what I'll ask for." I leaned back on the wall, propping a foot on one of his trembling knees. "I want you to restore the children of this town to the families you banished."

This got his attention. His black eyes darted up to meet mine at last. But instead of fear, it was hatred that burned there.

"They are better off without their parents." He cocked his head. "Those devil worshippers," he said, spitting a little with each word, "were unfit to raise even a mongrel dog, much less their ill-gotten progeny." The zeal of his hatred broke forth, and I finally saw the true face of the King Rat himself. "They all deserve to burn," he was yelling now. "Burn!"

I slapped him with the hard end of my flute case. My hands shook, and I knew the paint covering my face had begun to run with sweat. His tirade had unnerved me, but more than that, it ignited the purpose within me.

"Now," I said, breathing hard as I wiped spit and blood off the end of the case from where I'd split his lip. "I think you're forgetting who holds the upper hand."

The tip of his tongue worked along his lips, feeling for any loose teeth. He spat a glob of blood onto the floor, but his eyes remained crazed. "You'll pay for that," he promised.

I looked down on his prone form, wisps of white hair clung as flies buzzed around his eyes and ears, blood trickling from his mouth, glare full of an almost animal rage.

"Here's my offer: your life, as you know it, in exchange for this one good deed to counteract the scores of deaths you've caused."

"My life?" He grimaced. "Do you know what they do to murderers here?"

I shook my head. "I said your life as you *know* it. Do you think it's only animals who obey my music?" I waved my flute case at him.

His eyes widened, and his face grew ashen as he saw it close up. "You don't think I believe in that," he murmured, but his voice shook.

"You've seen this before, haven't you?" I breathed. "Perhaps long ago? Though it belonged to another at that time. A young woman who lived right here in this town."

For the first time, his mask of hatred fell apart, replaced by abject terror. "The witch sent you," he murmured.

"Now, I'll give you another chance. All you have to do is say *yes* or *no*."

"I grow tired of this." The Bishop's eyes were trained on the open flute case despite his words, and I could see him pulling together a plan. "I agree to whatever lunacy you ask," he said through gritted teeth the color of blood. "Just let me go."

"Not so easy as that." I smiled. "Swear it. Upon your blood." I held out my bone flute, the tip stained red with the blood-sworn oath from the Mayor.

His face twisted in incredulity.

"It seems you think I'm playing a game." I said pushing the flute toward his face. "Swear to your word."

"You're less than mad, I see that now. You're nothing but a fool," the Bishop said. He glared at me and then spat, a bloody globule hitting the pipe with a wet splat.

The room grew dim as if the clouds had covered the sun, and a frisson of energy passed between us. He swallowed nervously.

"That will do." I removed my foot, leaving a dirty smear across the front of his white cassock.

He sunk into the mire, stunned by the shock of power he'd just felt between us.

"I may be a fool," I said through gritted teeth. "But unlike you, I mean what I say. If you forfeit your promise, only ill fortune will come to you."

VI

Lucie

The first rabbit broke cover in the chill mist of twilight. My flute song thrilled a harmony along with its fast beating heart to lure her fellows from their warren. I could feel every fiber of the small beings held together with bone and sinew and something I could only think of as lifeblood. Soon, more brethren joined in, and by moonrise, I had a group of them hopping around a pitchfork in the central yard. I exhausted myself adding more and more rabbits until the song fell apart, and I collapsed back in the hayloft.

By the time spring had begun to blossom along the country lanes in earnest, under Aythe's tutelage, I'd become kith and kin with my new inheritance. The depth of my mother's flute-song pulled me in so that I had little time for anything else. My lips swelled and cracked from playing all hours of the day, and my fingers grew stiff. I slept with it pressed to my lips, like a lover and more, like my soul made real. It took me many sleepless nights to learn which song attracted which creature. Soon enough, I was calling shy deer from the forests and setting mice to dancing among the chaff.

"You're skin and bones." Tilo put a crock of thick cream and a hearth cake covered in hot jam before me. "Set that aside and eat or I swear I'll take the pipe from you."

I glared up at him, feeling every bit the wild nymph child that I must have seemed. The scent of the cream called to me, and I set to devouring the meal with both hands.

A raven landed in the doorway, clacking its beak. It dropped a single feather that shone purple in the dim light.

I glanced at Tilo who had stilled. "What does it mean?" I asked, licking jam from my fingers.

"Aythe wants to see us," he said.

"Why doesn't she just come here herself like she always does?"

"Her familiars are everywhere. And they watch. She must think you're ready. Or, at least that's what it looks like to me from the rabbit maypole I witnessed last night out in the fields." Pride and sorrow mingled in his gaze.

I returned his smile. "That was a good one," I admitted, feeling the sleepy contentment of a full belly and settling back in the chair. "The tune was just complex enough." I glanced at the feather. My blood hummed within me at the thought of Aythe and her steel gaze along with the rest of the Gathering. "When do we have to go?"

"Tonight. Something's happened in town. It must be bad if she's called the Gathering together."

I perked up from almost dozing. The town was a day's walk away and was the one place I hadn't been allowed to go near since our mother's death. "What do you think it is?"

He crouched to twirl the feather between his fingers, staring into the gloom settling along the fields. "There's talk that the White Bishop has returned."

"King Rat," I breathed and stood too quickly, toppling my stool. "I'll grab my hat."

The path deep into the forest had become even more overgrown through the seasons. But Tilo led me along each fork as surely as if it were leading us home. At the final bend, I smelled woodsmoke. Lights twinkled between the trees ahead, and we broke from the bracken into the sudden clearing of what looked to be a small village. Cottages clustered around a copse where livestock stood, penned in, with chickens wandering between the haystacks and woodpiles. A large cauldron sat out front of one house with sweet smelling smoke rising from it.

"What is this place?" I asked him, awed.

"You didn't think we lived up in the trees, did you?" Aythe said, coming down the path to meet us, a raven on her shoulder. "This is our home, where all exiles are welcome whether they follow the old ways or not. Tilo has been asked many a time to join us here."

I looked up at his scowl.

"We're fine on the farm, thank you," Tilo said.

"I'm glad you got our message all the same." Aythe smiled.

"Yes," he said. "What's going on? This isn't just about Lucie, is it?"

I looked around, noticing for the first time how many people there were. Rain began to fall as the circle gathered in the glade. There were more than before. Some of the newcomers were crying and most wore mismatched clothes not fit for the weather.

"What's going on," I whispered to Tilo. But it was Aythe who answered.

"The White Bishop is back in town, and his first order is a witch hunt."

Unease stirred within my chest, and my hand clutched at my flute case.

"Those under suspicion have been able to flee thus far but more are coming, and we have little room to hide them."

"What of their children?" Tilo asked, and I couldn't help but think of what it must have been like for him to flee at my age, to leave our mother behind to her fate in the town and start a new life without her.

Aythe met his gaze. "They were forced to stay behind by the Bishop."

"What, without their family?" someone asked.

She looked at me as she said, "He's taken as many as he can as oblates. The rest, we've heard, have escaped for now. But the guards aren't letting them leave."

"No," Tilo breathed.

I furrowed my brow. "Oblate?"

"The Church usually only takes in children who are orphans. They are raised in service to become clerics or monks. But it sounds like the Bishop is stealing them now...making orphans when he can't find enough otherwise."

"And the parents didn't stay behind to free them?" I asked, my voice rising .

A look of satisfaction flitted across Aythe's face at the passion in my question. "They had no choice," she said before she turned to the crowd. "Burnings, trials, inquisition...the Bishop has begun to unleash a reign of terror that is proving to eclipse the past horrors we'd all hoped were long gone."

"Surely in time we can go back," a woman broke in.

"The White Bishop is involved." Tilo said, his fists balled at his sides. "There's no returning."

My heart felt like it would break through my ribs, it beat so hard. "What do you plan to do?" I asked Aythe. "Or do you mean to let him burn more innocent people?"

Aythe smiled darkly, eyes only for me. "And what should we do?"

"Appeal to the Mayor?" someone spoke up.

"The White Bishop was careful who he targeted," a beleaguered man broke in. A filthy rag covered one side of his face, stiff with blood. "The Mayor won't go against the Bishop just for the likes of us."

"We can't let him win," a woman said, angry tears growing in her eyes.

"We can't fight him," another countered.

Aythe's gaze pierced me, that secret smile on her lips.

I piped up, cutting through the chatter. "I have an idea."

"Yes, Holda's daughter?" Aythe asked.

I pointed to the stream. "That runs down to the river and then on to town, doesn't it?" I pulled out my flute. "And rats can swim, can't they?"

Tilo squinted at me. "Lucie, nothing good ever comes from that mischievous look you get; the one I see in your eyes right now."

I grinned at him. "From what all the farmers who work the market say, it's only the richest houses that line the river. The manses are so large that you can't walk along the bridges without the guards giving you hassle."

"Yes, and the cathedral is right there on the river too." A wicked smile began to curve Aythe's lips showing every crooked tooth. "Let's see how the White Bishop fares with a pestilence of his own making."

VII

The Piper

It would seem that the Bishop had recovered quicker than I'd thought. Every spare guard within shouting distance had been notified once he'd divested himself of excrement. My motley surcote made for an especially easy target.

His men chased me. Their polished helms shone like mirrors in the sunlight. Moans of the sick grew sporadic the further I ran. And I realized I was lost. The map in my head of the wealthy river district spun, but my search for an inn last night had afforded me a reason to scour the streets for a way out of the guard's reach, knowing, eventually, that I'd find myself in a footrace. So I located a landmark I recognized.

I cut into the maze of alleys that made up the Tanners' Quarter. My plan to lead them away from the cathedral in a large loop had me giddy with anticipation, and I had to slow my breathing to keep from laughing as I ran. Cornering the Bishop had left me feeling more the Piper than ever. After so many careful months of planning, I'd finally seen fear wet the Bishop's eyes. At last, he'd known what I'd come for and all that I was capable of. And his oath colored my flute—his lifeblood.

The men took a wrong turn behind me, and I paused to lean within the shadow of a doorway. My breath came easier as I waited for them to realize their error and double back. I didn't want to get too far ahead and lose them only to circle around and find them regrouped in the central square. I laid my head back against the wooden door and smiled. The Bishop would've had to admit the truth upon calling the guard. A young traveling minstrel had gotten the upper hand while he squatted in the latrines. What I would have given to see that exchange. And it did more for my cause, defiling the Bishop's name amongst the townsfolk, than any proclamation on my part would've done. He'd be the talk of every tavern tonight as people laughed behind their mugs.

I made sure to lead the pack of guards past the best taverns the town had to offer, and the one old soldier that remained steadfast, I took to the outskirts on a chase amongst the rooftops. Unable to keep up, he huffed and puffed onto the curb, stripping helmet and surcote alike. Losing him was even easier as the townspeople wrapped up their chores for the day and crowded the streets to head to inns and taverns with gossip on their lips. I doubled back into the river district, sidestepping the busier streets and making my way to the central square.

The Mayor was right where I'd thought he'd be—in a spacious set of rooms on the third floor of his manse that he used to conduct his business. The slow dusk of an early summer night meant that the candles had yet to be lit. The whole house seemed to hold its breath, stilled by the gloaming.

I steeled myself for what was to come, shifting forward the part of me that was the Piper. I entered by way of the balcony, having shimmied up the drain pipe, and had the satisfaction of watching him jump as I said, "Good evening, Mayor."

"Piper," he hissed and stood, glancing at the empty door into the hallway.

I bowed slightly, knowing my grin must be ghastly with the cracked paint creasing my cheeks from the day's sweaty chase.

He leaned forward on the desk between us. "Half the city guard is looking for you! Did you really try to kill the Bishop?"

"Is that the story he's spouting?" I scoffed and then couldn't help but ask, "Tell me, was there any mention of a latrine?"

The Mayor tensed, anger growing hot in what little of his face I could see above his beard. "We had a deal, Piper."

"Yes," I said, flicking a bell on my cap. "And I told you the Bishop and I have business of our own."

"If you keep threatening him," he said, his voice gruff, "then you'll get caught and quartered before you can fulfill our bargain."

I danced forward to shut the door. "And how would this bargain of ours fair if the town were to learn of it?"

He arched an eyebrow.

I opened my hands and walked toward him, just out of reach. "The Mayor employs a mad minstrel who then tries to kill the Bishop." I wagged a finger. "Not very good for business."

He paled. "Tell me, why shouldn't I just have you killed right now?"

"I knew your word alone wouldn't hold you. And so here's your incentive." I pulled out the flute with its carving, smeared red with his blood as well as that of the Bishop's, and laid my lips against the mouthpiece.

He jumped back as if pricked by the first notes, feeling the pull of the magic there tug at his lifeblood.

"That is but a taste of your song." I stepped forward and the Mayor took a step back. "If you so much as speak against me, you'll learn the full breadth of my skill."

My skin prickled as the door creaked open behind me.

"Papa?" I heard a young voice say, as shrill as a reed pipe.

The Mayor's eyes grew wide, and I turned slowly. There, standing in the crack of the door, was a girl. She was about half my age with the same dark hair as her father though hers was unruly, tied up within a white scarf that was coming loose to show black ringlets.

"Gertrude," the Mayor choked out. "What are you doing out of bed?"

"I heard a song," she said, looking between us, dazed. "It spoke to me."

The Mayor stepped between us, pushing her gently out. "It was nothing," he said quietly to her. "You go back to bed, and I'll send warm milk up in a moment."

She gave me one last lingering look that pierced through my Piper facade and cut me to the quick before she turned away.

The Mayor shut the door behind her, pausing with his back to me.

"Her mother was...?" I found myself asking, thinking back to what the red innkeeper had told me. "She held to the old beliefs?"

"Is that why she heard your song?" he asked, his voice soft with defeat.

"The song called to her because she has your blood," I said. "She's tied to you. If you fail, that means she'll pay as you do."

He didn't turn, but I could almost see how my words were clicking into place.

"I told you when we first spoke." I backed to the balcony. "I keep my promises, and I always take what I'm owed."

"And when do you plan on fulfilling your promise?" he ground out. "When will you get rid of the rats?"

"Soon, but I came here tonight because I need something."

"Oh?" He turned finally, his eyebrows rising in mock surprise. His voice took on some of its steel from earlier. "Changing the bargain already?"

"No change." I shook my head. "Just make sure there are no guards at the western gates tonight."

He looked at me from the corners of his eyes, but asked no more questions. Perhaps he thought he would soon get what he wanted either way—my head or a scapegoat.

"Think of it as done. We're short on guards anyways, what with the hunt for you and the barracks overrun with vermin."

"Good. Listen for my song at moonrise." I stepped back up onto the balcony ledge and dropped into the alley below.

I crept away, close to the walls to keep my bells from echoing. The soft footsteps of someone following me stilled my heart. My fingers tightened on my flute, but before I could bring it to my lips, a voice whispered, "You're the Piper aren't you?"

I whirled and was once again looking down on the Mayor's young daughter.

"Gertrude," I whispered in surprise. I glanced behind her, but we were very much alone and out of sight of the manse, around the next bend behind a cobbler's shop. "You should be back in bed."

"I heard you and Papa talking," she said, undeterred. "You spoke about Mama."

My blood ran cold, and I swallowed, thinking back to what I'd said. "Did I?"

"He won't tell me about her." Her brows knitted. "Did you know her?" she asked.

"I didn't," I admitted and then at the sadness that clouded the girl's eyes I said, "But I'm a follower of the old ways as she was."

Her mouth formed an *oh* of shock. "But Papa said we can't say that. The Bishop will steal me away like he did the other children."

I kneeled, meeting her eyes. "The other children?" I asked.

And she nodded. "The witch kids."

I felt my heart skip a beat. "Gertrude, do you know where they're being kept?"

A grin lit up the young face, her eyes growing mischievous. "I visit them sometimes, even though I'm not supposed to. But Alf's there, and I want to make sure he's okay."

I swallowed, trying to remain calm. "Would you tell me how to get there?"

She pursed her lips.

"I know it's dangerous," I hedged. "But I want to see Alf too, and the others. I think I can make sure they're safe, like you do."

That seemed to sway her. She told me the route and her secret way of getting in. I sent her back off to bed before the Mayor could miss her, watching from around the corner as her small figure disappeared inside. I let out a long breath and climbed the nearest drain onto a gutter before scrambling up onto the chimney top to survey the town. There, a block away, just as she'd said, sprawled the roof of the old mill and from within its high windows a faint light shone.

VIII

Lucie

The first rat was the hardest to collect.

I went from house to house in our village on the edge of the forest, playing in the dead of night so softly that only they could hear me. But the village rats were all happily nestled between the cottage eaves and well-thatched roofs so that none stirred for too long. On my third night, I became frustrated at my lack of control over the flute's power and tapped into that anger. The heat of the emotion flowed through me, blocking out all thought and leading to a heady sense of scorn and power. I placed my lips to the flute mouth.

The song that rose out into the night jarred and screeched. I felt the creatures begin to bend to my will but not out of harmony between two living beings. Instead, shadows rose as if shackled around me, cavorting and pulling at the rats in their nearby nests. I felt power grow inside me like a darkness that seeped into my very bones, clouding my vision with black promises. I broke off at once, gasping in the cool night air. The few rats that had been nearby scurried off. I ran to the nearest window and watched as my eyes returned from their hollow black stare back to the deep brown and white they'd always been.

Shaking, I returned to the path that led home.

I slid down the sign post at the edge of our farm to crouch in the dirt, unable to face Tilo's questioning gaze tonight. I could still feel the dark power seeping into the tip of my tongue. The flute glistened in the moonlight. I couldn't stand it in my hands any longer, but still it took every fiber of my control to carefully replace it in its case.

What had once felt like a gift—to discover that my mother's flute matched the longing deep within—now felt like a curse. I was failing not only Aythe and the children of the town, but my mother's memory. At the first sign of difficulty, I'd called up the darkness of our talent and used it to do my bidding. I pulled my cap down against my ears, shutting my eyes tight as if I could keep the despair at bay.

Shame kept me apart from my brother as I did my chores in silence for the next fortnight. Tilo didn't ask why I no longer went into the village to play for the rats. I knew he hoped in his secret heart that my plan would fail, that I could remain here, safe under his watchful gaze.

One night, close to dawn, I was sitting on the fence when I noticed a small creature watching me from the corner of the grain shed. I'd been contemplating how Aythe would take it when she learned my plan had fallen apart. I began to hum to myself. I hadn't played my mother's flute since the song of dancing shadows. It had been the longest I'd gone without playing since I could remember. My reed pipe had always been in my hand or pocket even before.

I sat up, focusing on this runt of a rat. Something reached out and touched me from behind its dark eyes. It felt like the brush of two kindred spirits, set apart from others. I found myself wanting to connect with the lonely creature.

My fingers found the flute case I still carried in a breast pocket close to my heart. I took it out slowly, watching the rat, and began to play a song just for us; a song of un-belonging and raw need for something more. It crept closer, and I could see just how scrawny he was. When I stopped my song, he stayed by my side, and I spoke softly to him.

"How are you doing, small one?"

He cocked his head.

"I have a tune that will perk you up." And then I played a melody that came from my heart. It spoke of finding a purpose, of a story left untold, and of a hero made to finish it.

The rat ran up my leg and onto my shoulder where it listened in that special way animals have that tells you, *we are in this together*.

"With your help, I think we can do this." I smiled. "Every hero needs a name. How about Wiglo? That seems to suit you."

The rat perked up, standing on its hind legs, its small front paws clasped together as if to say, *yes, that sounds like me!*

After a day together, I could send Wiglo here and there to do small tasks with a single whistled note. It mesmerized me, the change in the tune that could persuade him to run about. Once I was sure of him, I set off for the Gathering. I fastened my cloak about my shoulders and Wiglo climbed up into the hood so that he wouldn't be flung off as I raced into the woods.

Ravens circled above us as we made our way into the forest and, as always, Aythe stepped out from behind a tree when I neared the southern glade. The woods were her front doorstep.

"Hello, Lucie," she said, and we walked together into the small town of the Gathering folk.

"I did it," I huffed, breathless.

She looked at Wiglo who had climbed onto my shoulder to look around, and she smiled. "I see. When will the others be ready to join him?"

I shook my head. "Soon. But I thought of a problem."

"Ah, did you now?" A hint of a smile winked in her eyes.

"Yes. What happens when the plague takes hold and they lock everyone in? I heard that happened to a town on the coast, and no one survived."

"Very good," she murmured. "You're as smart as your brother."

I quirked an eyebrow. "Tilo?" I knew my brother was stubborn and resourceful, but I'd never thought of him as *smart*.

"Non-gentry are often overlooked in that way," she said, beckoning me to sit on a stump at the edge of the clearing. "A noble can be book-learned and become all kinds of things: cleric, merchant, mayor." She said the last as if it were a bitter curse. "But a peasant who outsmarts a noble can only be described one way...witch."

I thought about the sting of bitterness in her words. I had little cause to interact with nobles. None lived in our village and even the town had few that kept a crest and title. But Aythe had lived many more years than I had and knew things I realized that I could not yet fathom. "And that's what happened to my mother?" I heard myself ask.

She cocked her head. "You're more like your mother than you know," she murmured and I felt my heart stutter in response.

"What was she like?" I asked, my voice quiet despite the hectic pace of my heart.

Aythe's steel gaze turned soft for the first time since I'd known her. She took my hand in hers, looking at the pipe I held there, and she spoke. "No matter how bad things got, how mean and hateful people became near the end, she somehow always found small ways to spread joy in the world. Not a day goes by that I don't wish it had been me on that pyre instead of her."

"You knew her well, then?"

Aythe let out a hoarse laugh, her throat tight from what looked to be unshed tears. "Close as two souls can get."

I opened my mouth to ask more, but the sorrow between us was already too much for me to bear.

"So," she began. "How would you solve the problem of rampant plague if you were a noble?"

I hesitated. I could see that she was testing me. Aythe was nothing if not prepared, and I hadn't forgotten how she'd asked me just the right questions to make me speak up in the Gathering with my plan for the rats. I swallowed. "Only I could stop the rats once they'd entered and begun their work."

"Yes." She nodded. "And how would you get into the town unseen? A girl running around, playing her flute and dancing with plague rats would attract all kinds of attention."

"I could do it at night," I offered. "I'm good at keeping to the shadows."

"Or," she said, pulling a sheaf of paper from her cloak, "no more hiding what you can do." She handed me the page, watching for my reaction from beneath hooded eyes.

I took the paper, shaking a little under the feeling of being watched by her, of trying to live up to all she expected of me as Lucie the daughter of Holda.

My mind spun as I looked at the picture on the paper. "Tell me more," I breathed.

From within a bag at her hip, she removed a long pair of scissors and a jester's cap tipped with silver bells. "I'll do you one better. Let me show you."

✦

"I see you've gotten the knack of it now." Tilo leaned against the chicken coop, both of us watching Wiglo collect eggs by pushing them in a run toward the basket, much to the chagrin of the chickens.

I broke off playing and grinned as my small friend kept at it. "Now we just need hundreds of others."

"Or a thousand," Tilo countered.

I scratched my head carefully beneath my cap, making sure to keep it from revealing too much of what lay underneath. I knew the time had come to tell him of my plan. "The only problem would be stopping the town from being shut down when it's overrun with vermin."

Tilo looked at me confused.

"And how do we get the Bishop to agree to reunite the children with their families? If it gets too out of hand, the Mayor would have to close the city gates, quarantine the whole town."

Tilo crossed his arms over his chest. "So this is why you've been disappearing to the woods now. You and Aythe have been trying to come up with something?"

"Perhaps she already has," I wheedled, knowing he wasn't going to like what I was about to propose. "What if I were to go in after them. The rats I mean. I could convince the Mayor and the Bishop that it was in the best interest of everyone to—"

"Absolutely not." Tilo was shaking his head. "You haven't been there since..." he broke off before he could say, *since mama was burned at the stake.* He swallowed. "You haven't been there since you were small. You know nothing about how places like that work. Have you thought about how you would even get close to them? These are the most powerful men in the whole county. They'll be surrounded by every kind of protection."

I held up my flute. "I could disguise myself as a traveling musician. They can get in anywhere."

He looked between my grin and our mother's flute. "A minstrel? You?" He laughed. "They'd know you for just another country girl in a heartbeat."

"Not if I look the part." I pulled the cap from my head.

"Aythe cut your hair." His jaw clenched and he made to throw the feed pail he held before taking a deep breath. "Lucie," he said, voice careful to disguise his anger. "This isn't a game. It'll take more than a haircut to turn you into a minstrel."

"I know," I said, feeling hot around the ears. "There's more." From my case, I took out the posting I'd been carrying for the few days since speaking with Aythe and handed it to him.

He unscrolled it to reveal a jester dressed all in motley, face painted, and dancing about. His eyebrows rose before shutting down into a scowl. "And Aythe is putting you up to this?"

"No, it's my plan too." I shook my head, trying not to let my cheeks heat up with the shame of having a secret as big as this. But, then again, hadn't he been the one to start this masquerade of *it's for your own good* by hiding my birthright from me in the first place?

"You're too young," he pleaded. "You know nothing of townsfolk like the ones who run that place."

I straightened, feeling the fear building in my chest. Tilo had a way of talking me out of my mischief before it even began. But I couldn't let him talk me out of this. "Aythe has told me everything about the Bishop and the Mayor that I need to know. Tilo, she trusts me, and so should you."

"I do trust you. It's her I don't trust." He sighed, eyeing my shorn hair. "Did you ask Aythe how she knows so much about them?" My brother's voice was so small I could barely hear it among the clucking squabbles of the hens. "Or why she'll stop at nothing to get vengeance?"

I shook my head slowly but thought again about her words that she wished she'd been on my mother's pyre instead. "She's the leader; it's her job to care about the witch hunt."

"Aythe is not just the leader of the Gathering." He widened his eyes as if I should guess at what was coming next. "She is...she is our mother's twin, Lucie."

"What?" I asked, feeling confused and wary, again. There was no way that the tall, gray-haired witch that seemed to be made of nothing more than cold anger and ravensong was our mother's twin.

Tilo nodded, watching me. "Aythe fled here, to our old family farm when things started getting worse for her in town. She thought that we would be safe in town because everyone loved mama so much. *Holda, you're the best midwife we have—the whole town will fight for you,* I remember her saying on the night she fled. *But no one cares for a spinster woman like me; smarter than half the guild members here and getting richer by the day for it too.*" Tilo paused, swallowing hard before continuing. "Mama was taken late one night as she returned home from helping a woman who'd delivered a stillbirth. The woman died. The next morning, they burned her at the stake."

I was shaking my head now, fighting back the overwhelming sense of betrayal and sorrow that rose up for a mother I could barely even remember.

"When Aythe found out what had happened, she snuck into the town and carved a curse onto the Bishop's door, banishing him for as long as our mother's gift went unused. *The price of Holda's death,* she'd said."

I looked down at the flute in my hands. "This flute...that was the gift Aythe's curse spoke of. And the White Bishop had stayed away all these years. Tilo, he only returned within a few weeks of me learning to play it." I squinted, trying to think.

Tilo nodded.

"Then why did Aythe force you to give the flute to me if it was the only thing keeping the Bishop away?"

He finally met my eyes. "All I know is that Aythe has been following the White Bishop from town to town all these years, unable to get close to him. He knows her face and keeps himself surrounded by men who would burn a witch quicker than spitting. So, why did our aunt give up hunting him and return here?" Tilo shrugged. "Perhaps he was growing too old, and she wanted her vengeance before he died. Or perhaps, she was telling the truth when she met you that night, and she wants nothing more than for you to fulfill your birthright."

I mulled this over, thinking of my aunt's hardened gaze anytime she spoke of the King Rat. "Perhaps both," I said.

"If you're not careful, Lucie, you'll be sucked into this until you're as bitter and angry as she is."

I tensed. "He burned our mother," I said, my voice hoarse from the strain of not shouting. "And I won't run and hide like you did. Not this time."

His eyes widened with shock. "I told her you were too young for this!"

"Too young?" I shook my head, trying to make sense of all that I felt. "How could you lie about who Aythe is to us? I thought all of our family had died! I thought we were all alone!"

"Lucie," he murmured, brow creasing. "I was afraid. You don't know her like I do. Aythe will do anything for vengeance." He straightened, meeting my eyes. "And you're a lot like her."

"What is that supposed to mean?" I scoffed, but his words had chilled me. Already I'd felt less and less like my old self, becoming something darker with edges sharper than they seemed.

"If you're not careful, all this truth will burn you up inside."

"Truth is power, Tilo." At that moment, I wanted nothing more than the power to leave here and fulfill what I knew was inside me.

He sighed and tried to ruffle my hair like he always had.

I pulled back, glaring.

His smile was sad. "Just remember, if it ever gets too hard, think about what kind of song mama would want played in the world."

IX

The Piper

I set off in the direction Gertrude had pointed out to me. The old mill had been built on a small island between the refectory and a tributary of the river. Abandoned over the winter after a particularly bad harvest with not enough hands to work it, the low stone building had high windows. A perfect place to keep stolen children.

The secret entrance the Mayor's daughter had described lay in shadow, almost at the bottom of the building. A warm draft around my ankles was the only sign, and I never would have found it if not for her directions. The church bell tolled ten, and I patted my flute case out of habit. Time to get to work.

I bent down and crawled through the gap in the back of the building that had once been used to sluice chaff from the stone floor. I felt my hips catch for a second in the narrow hole and kept myself from panicking with a few steady breaths before wriggling free. I crouched behind what looked to be the remnants of the large miller's wheel. It blocked this part of the building from the rest which explained why none had tried to crawl out.

Two long rows of beds lined the left hand wall where the children slept in twos and threes, huddled together. The nearest one woke as I leaned forward, and I shushed him into silence.

"I'm here from the Gathering," I whispered, and the little boy perked up.

"Is my family okay?" he asked.

I nodded, not knowing which were his people but hoping they were amongst the ones who'd arrived safely. "They sent me to make sure you're well. Are you being fed?" I looked him over for signs of violence or neglect but the small boy seemed less dirty and better clothed than the street children.

The boy shrugged. "We have to learn chants for the choir and some of us are being trained to fight. If we don't want to fight, we get punished. Sometimes lashings, sometimes no meals."

I bit my lip. "Do what they ask of you, for now. I promise to end this all soon."

He nodded, his face tightening with purpose. "I knew they'd send someone. They wouldn't leave us here. The ravens told us."

"Good boy. Tell the others. The Piper's come to help."

I slipped away and walked along the riverbank, down in the shadows of the quay walls, feeling like my heart was torn out and left behind with the children. A few rats followed me but most kept to their tasks of running amok in the manses and cathedral. "Tonight's the night, chaps. Ready to go back home?" I murmured.

The moon had cleared the few clouds and was shining brightly along the eastern horizon. I knelt by the river and scrubbed the paint from my face. I wanted to be myself for what I was about to do or to be as close to that lost, motherless child that was Lucie as I could get. My heart hammered with anticipation as I began to remove the bells from my ankles. I set them along with my hat in a rocky crevice there within the wall before ascending the stairs up and out of the river.

No one was out in the square at the center of town, the night air thick with the heat of a summer's day still burning off the cobblestones. The belfry loomed above me, and it felt as if time stood still, each footfall hemmed in a cloak of shadow, and the moon's glow fell silvery bright amongst the folds of my motley. Even I would have doubted that I was little more than a fantom. Except the fierce beating of my heart would not let me drift off into unreality. I patted my flute case. I was here for a purpose, and the very air in my lungs tasted sweet with the portent of victory. All my planning and practice and careful thought wound up in this moment.

I dipped into the shadows of the stables to watch the rectory. His was one of the few windows on the second floor still lit with candlelight, the other master clerics having absconded at his arrival or been carried off by the flux. The pale form stood out in its white cassock as he snuffed the candles one by one. When all was darkness within, I sidled forward beneath the eaves, borrowing a few bales of straw from the stables to place below his window.

"What are you doing?" a voice asked, too loud in the quiet of the night.

I spun, thinking of guards, but it was the young stablehand, Adelbert, standing there, curiosity and a tinge of confusion on his face.

"You scared me," I whispered, looking around. We were still alone. "I could ask the same about you. It's late."

"I sleep with the horses. I heard what you did to the Bishop." He crossed his arms. "You shouldn't be here."

I thought of reaching for my flute, of using it to make him help me. Instead, I took a deep breath and gambled on my intuition. "Look," I said. "You're one of only a few people I've met in this town that even seems to care what's happening."

His face tensed into a scowl. "What do you mean?"

"I mean," I said and pointed to the old mill behind us, "that the Bishop has a whole village worth of children locked up not two hundred paces from where he gives his sermons."

The boy's scowl shifted to a grimace that looked very much like guilt.

"You knew," I said. "And you've done nothing to help them?"

"They're safer there than on the streets," he said quietly.

"Is that what he tells people?"

Adelbert shifted uncomfortably.

"He's training them to fight," I whispered, stepping closer. "Or did he not make that clear either? He's always wanted more power."

"Look, even if I did want to help, anyone who gets in his way disappears."

I nodded. "I know. And I'm here to put an end to that."

His brows knitted and his gaze flicked around, looking to see if I carried a weapon.

I waved a hand. "It's not what you think. But you don't have to do anything except go back to the stables and pretend you never saw me."

Adelbert opened his mouth but then glanced in the direction of the mill. He nodded. As I turned away, he said quietly, "Are they alive, the children's parents?"

Without turning back, I nodded. "Yes, they're safe. And I'm not leaving here without what I came for."

After a moment I heard his heavy footfalls retreat back to the hay loft, and I settled my mind back into the task at hand.

The low stone crenellations afforded an easy climb up onto the roof of the rectory. I was able to slip along silently, now that I was free from my belled ankles and hat, until I reached the largest window. The latch proved easy to flip with the needle I kept within my case, and I stepped inside. I whistled a few notes and rats scurried out to surround me, surveying the dark room with its central large bed. Soft snores rose and fell from within the velvet hangings. I couldn't help myself. I padded over and, using my flute, parted the curtains to peer within.

The waxy nose of the Bishop peeked out from a thin coverlet, a skull cap atop his head. I brushed the hair from my eyes as I watched him. Even in sleep, he seemed somehow less than a man. Sallow skin stretched tight over sharp cheekbones and sunken eyes. Skeletal, I remembered what Tilo had said to me in the woods that fateful night. Hate consumed as surely as the flux.

It was my rats that woke him as they climbed up to nibble at an ear.

"Shush," I coaxed as he startled awake and began to flail. Rats scattered.

He spluttered, catching sight of my head poking into his curtains. "Angel?" His voice, made small by fear, spoke of his guilt. My flaxen hair backlit by the moonlight streaming from the open window—I must look like an avenging angel to this man roused from nightmares.

His eyes too betrayed him, wide with fear, and it was then that I knew for sure. This man expected to be damned. The weight of all the men and women he'd named 'witch' and sentenced to burn would weigh heavy on a single soul.

"I'm no angel," I murmured, pulling back the curtains and standing to my full height.

Now that he saw my motley surcote, he sat up, scrambling back against his headboard. "You!"

"I've come to call in your promise," I said, holding up my flute with his blood still staining it. "Allow the exiled peoples to return to their homes. If not for them, then for their children's sake."

He shook his head, eyeing the flute. "I can't give you what you ask."

"Can't means won't. I told you this before, Bishop, I'm not playing a game. Either you remove the sentence of exile from the innocent people and reunite them with their children, or I take that power out of your hands."

"You'll never get what you want, not so long as I'm alive."

A sly smile formed along my lips. "I was hoping you'd say that."

"You said you're no murderer."

"I'm not, but you are. Let's find out what your song sounds like, King Rat."

The rats around us stood up on their back legs, testing the air with their sensitive noses. With a deep breath, I brought my flute up to my lips. The first note rang out just as the Bishop threw back his bedsheets and parted his lips to yell for the guards waiting down the hall. His gaping mouth yawned there, silent as his ears caught the melody. He stilled. The notes took hold of something deep within him and squeezed.

The Bishop's song spun out soft and strong as a thread of silk, so quick that it took hold before he could move. I watched in the half light of the moon. He grew rigid as he listened, mouth agape to show missing teeth amidst the glimmering wetness of a tongue at work. Trying to yell or sing or laugh, I was unsure. But I knew what magic was working within him. His song was unlike any I'd attempted to play before. People had different motivations than animals, as a rule, and I'd never had a reason to cross that line.

The sweet tang of the blood oath on my tongue, as I drew the power of it in and played the notes into the room, filled me with the knowing of him.

The Bishop's melody was caustic and filled with the jangling notes of a minor harmony until I got it under control. Dissonance paired with a steadfast march until it held an uncanny resemblance to a funeral dirge—as if the joys of life itself had been found lacking, and all that remained were the lowest of notes.

I felt something shift within me as my fingers moved across the flute holes. A barrier I'd felt only once before gave way until the force of the song filled me. I hungered for more. It was kin to what I'd felt on that first shadowed night at home when I'd played for control amongst the rats. Sweat broke out on my upper lip as I fought the hunger.

As if on strings, the Bishop jolted forward, stiff at first in his acquiescence. I felt my own heart strain at the darkness that was using the blood oath to control him. But once the song took hold, his steps lightened, head leaning forward, and they became one—the flute song and his dance. I played him through the window and out onto the sill where he dropped heavily onto the pile of straw I'd arranged earlier. He lay there, chaff covering his cassock and sticking out of his nightcap. I landed easily with the power still flowing through me, one hand playing along, next to him. And then he righted himself, and we were off.

I collected my rats as I went. They poured from the gutters and fell from the eaves in droves, crawling amongst each other as a moving wall of fur and whiskers. The pattering of their feet through the detritus of the river district grew so loud as to become a part of the song I played, a harmony of clicking nails and long tails, glistening with the promise of a growing plague. Townspeople roused and dashed out of doors before quickly jumping up onto rain barrels and tables, anything they could use to put distance between them and the horde of rats. Nobles and merchants leaned out of windows only to have rats fall from eaves above onto their heads and run down the balconies to join the procession.

Their screams added to my song.

We passed a pile of bodies, caked in fresh lye. Ravens had been at work on eyes and lips. I almost stopped playing with the stench filling my nose and mouth. I had done this. Eyeless sockets stared into me, gored mouths cut into a black grin. Amongst the pile, movement. As one, a horde of my vermin friends left the plague corpses along the gutters to follow me back home.

Rats, beasts of filth and wits, never ceased to amaze me. Dancing past the dead had helped dampen the dark power surging through me.

And so I played the Bishop into a funeral march into the town square before me. He was King Rat indeed, fully in his element scampering along with them, wild gleam of greed and hunger in his shining eyes. His nightcap had come askew and the cassock untied at the neck to reveal the sunken chest beneath. And yet he grinned, showing his true nature, sly and full of his own might.

I had him crouch in the shadows of the gate leading out of the square before I turned in a slow circle, still playing. My melody wove in a higher pitch on every alternate harmony until the skittering of rat paws on cobblestones nearly drowned out my playing. I glanced up to see the lone silhouette of the Mayor come out onto his balcony, drawn by the promise of my song. He still wore his suit of black. It would seem he'd kept his doors open to see if I'd actually fulfill my promise. I had never fully trusted him, but his curiosity seemed to play into my hands tonight all the same.

I flourished into a dance under his gaze and had the rats circling around me in concentric rings like gears behind a clock. And then they broke as I ran forward, hopping, leaping among them, and they scurried after me toward the bridge leading out of town. Even more villagers popped their heads out of windows, half asleep, eyes wide in shock. Those not screaming as rat upon rat threw themselves from the rooftops and drainpipes to run around me, were pointing and gawking at the Bishop as he danced along at the front of the horde just behind me, King Rat himself.

Sweating and breathing hard between notes, we cavorted out through the richest parts of town, along the avenues lined with statues and flickering light posts. My legs grew stiff, and my fingers ached, but still we danced toward the West gate.

The archway leading out to the main road stood empty, as the Mayor had promised, and I ran out into the stillness of the countryside with the horde of rats and their King trailing frantically along. A crowd had gathered behind us; the townspeople from the river district; a scattering of nobles wrapped in robes; half-asleep servants and cooks; and the few of the city guard who were sober enough to stand at this hour of the night with mugs of mead still in hand.

The church bell tolled midnight as they gathered by the gate, watching the Piper lead the parade of rats out of town with King Rat frolicking in the lead. I heard, on the breeze, the faint sound of applause.

X

Lucie

As we neared the stone bridge, I looked back, the town lights as distant as fireflies among the hills. The rats parted around Aythe as she walked toward us across the bridge, shuttered lantern swaying from her walking staff. She danced along with my melody, not gracefully like a reed in the wind, but raucously until the rats leapt about her in glee. Ravens circled above to add their cries to the night. The part of me that had come alive as I plied the strings of the Bishop's broken blood oath writhed with yearning. It was like being caught in the fury of a storm.

Together we danced, circling the Bishop. I lost myself to the power of it. The only thing holding me to earth was the song and the gleam of hunger in my aunt's eyes. She grinned and kicked out, sending the Bishop reeling.

The reverie broke. I took my mouth away from the flute to lick my cracked lips watching her sing the fading chords to the song as if she were a child of the night itself, one with the moon and stars. My breath hitched with the knowing of her magic. I'd never seen her open up fully before, and it hit me with a sense of awe and not a little fear.

At my side, the Bishop fell amongst the squeaking of hundreds of rats. He closed his eyes and put his face into his hands, sobbing now that he had been released.

Aythe's eyes glinted as she watched me. "Good evening, Lucie."

"Good evening, Aunt," I rasped, breathing hard and unsure if I would be able to stand for much longer. She handed me her stick, and I leaned on it with all my weight, glad for the support.

Aythe turned to him. "Hello, King Rat."

He peered up at her through the slits in his fingers and scrambled back, hissing. "I should have known it was you behind this witchery, devil," he groaned, exhaustion keeping him from saying more.

"Ah, so the memory of me has not yet fled your slow wits, I see." She took the lantern from her stick and unshuttered it to have a better look at him.

His pallid face turned up to hers. "How could I forget you," he said, a trickle of blood seeping from the corner of his mouth. "Using your sordid friendship with the Mayor's young wife to gain his ear."

"I think you've forgotten your role in this," Aythe mused, fury behind her eyes. "You turned everything good in our town, everything sacred into nothing more than a holy game."

He sneered. "One that you happily played. You are, after all, the one who used your dark magic to curse the abbott. There wouldn't have even been a witch hunt if not for you!"

I blinked at this, expecting Aythe to laugh at his lies.

Instead she grimaced, lips drawing back into a snarl as she said, "I didn't hear you complaining at the time, or have you forgotten that's the only reason you became Bishop in the first place."

I frowned at their words. Tired as I was, it was difficult to keep track of their meaning. I looked between the White

Bishop kneeling on the roadside and my aunt, sneering down at him. She looked every part the demon he named her to be with her white curls flying around her face and only the lantern and moon above to light her.

"What does he mean?" I found myself asking into the quiet of the night. "You didn't start the witch hunt, you weren't even in town."

He croaked a laugh. "She was there for the first hunt, all those years ago. Right in the center of it. Weren't you?"

Without looking at me, she answered. "Yes. We were promised sanctuary, kinship, a place to belong in town. And we would have had it if you hadn't been so greedy."

My heart skipped a beat as I looked between them.

The Bishop's mouth twisted. "I hardly think you're one to talk about greed." He turned his head so that his bloodied lips caught the glint of the lamplight. "How do you think she's survived all these years on the road? There's money in curses, child."

"Aythe?" I asked, trying to keep my heart from rending into a thousand tiny pieces.

Her eyes snapped to mine but lost none of their sharpness. "Who do you think pays for the Gathering?" she asked, that sneer still in her voice that I'd heard on our first meeting. "There'd be no survivors if not for me."

I thought back to the small village in the woods, its cookfires and goats and hidden meadows. And then I thought of the Bishop's accusation. *Curses, money, greed...*

"And perhaps none know what they survived was your doing," the Bishop said.

I felt the tip of my already dry tongue split until I tasted metal as I bit down on it to keep from crying out in shock.

She glared at him. "Well, now that we have the true measure of each other, it's time for you to take your proper place in the world. That is, after all, the very thing you've been clawing after all along, now isn't it?" Her smile broke forth, sharp with promise.

Leaning on the staff and breathing hard, I watched my aunt. The two were old friends turned bitter enemies. My head swam.

Aythe drew a red velvet sash from around her waist and tied it in a blindfold around the Bishop.

"What is this?" he wheezed and then his voice quaked as he shouted. "Aren't you going to kill me, or do I have to kneel here until I die of exposure?"

"No," she crooned, the fire of vengeance burning in her eyes. "You should know better than to think that of such a one as I."

"Then why blindfold me, coward?"

"For once, you see the truth of the matter. I used to be a coward," she agreed. "I fled when I should have stayed and fought for my way of life and for my sister, for my people."

The Bishop's thin lips drew together into an evil, jeering smile beneath the blindfold. "But instead, you ran!"

"Yes."

"And you left her to be burned in your stead!"

Aythe dropped down into a crouch so quickly that I took a step back. She watched him closely. Her gaze filled with a hunger that had the hairs standing up on the back of my neck.

"Tell me," she whispered. "Did you know it was Holda tied there when you set the pyre alight? Or, did you think it was me you'd finally caught after all those nights of searching?"

His mouth twisted into a frown, and I held my breath, waiting and watching for the answer that would shape my own past and future. "I knew it must be you leaving the Mayor's house," he whispered, but even to my own ears he sounded unsure. "You always visited his wife in the dead of night."

"Matilda," she breathed. "Say her name, Rat."

His mouth drew into a thin line. "She died that night, or did you not know?"

I saw a flicker of pain cross Aythe's eyes. "I knew," she murmured. "In childbirth. Holda was there as midwife. But couldn't save her."

I blinked. "The Mayor's wife," I whispered, thinking back to the young girl called to her father's room by the song of his blood. "Her daughter was named Gertrude. I met her. She spoke of her mother as one of us."

Aythe looked back to the Bishop. "Does the Mayor know that you burned the midwife that saved his daughter's life?"

"What difference does it make," he growled.

"See," she said. "The scum can't even admit he burned the wrong sister."

A low chuckle resounded from the Bishop that had my fists balled in anger. "All you devil witches are one in the same," he spat.

"So it is true, King Rat. You thought she was me." Aythe's eyelids fluttered, and I felt hot angry tears slide down my own cheeks. "But you have it right, in a way. We witches are of one spirit. When you cut one of us down, another will spring up, twice as strong. We will not be silenced, especially not by the likes of you."

Aythe knelt before him and began to hum the melody from the song we three had danced to, the very one that had brought him out of his bed and far from the city. He, blindfolded, turned here and there as if he were a starving man smelling a freshly-baked pie on the wind. Aythe unwound a cord of braided rope that she'd had looped around her neck and began to bind his wrists with one end. He strained to stay balanced while Aythe pulled him upright with a quick jerk on her end of the rope. He tottered for a breath and then took one step forward and another on bare feet, trailing after her humming melody.

"What about the children?" I called to her. "They're still imprisoned by the Bishop's guard."

"Oh, my dear Lucie," she said, her voice singing the words. "I have faith you'll get them out."

My stomach dropped, realizing, from everything I'd heard this night, that my brother had been right. My aunt was not the woman I'd thought her to be, not the leader I'd hoped she was. And she was nothing like my mother. "You're not coming back?"

"You have your mother's flute, what need do you have of me?" she asked. She reached forward, as if to pat my cheek.

But I took a step back.

Her face creased in anger before it smoothed again, and she grasped her staff that I held before me.

I pulled it so that she had to take a step forward, coming in close. Her smell of belladonna and the earthy scent of the acorns she kept in her pockets for the crows enveloped me. "You're right" I said, my voice thick, my eyes never leaving hers. "I have outgrown your vengeance."

Her hooded gaze softened. "In these many months of showing you the power you could hold with your gift, I've always known you are more like her than you will ever resemble me."

I swallowed, and she leaned her forehead against mine. My eyes closed, tears spilling out.

"Lucie, I have failed in so many things." Her voice broke. "I will not fail you by remaining here."

I shook my head. "I would not allow you to stay," I said, trembling from head to toe but steadfast, "not even if you wished to."

She smiled, and I choked back a sob. The sorrow in her eyes, so very much like Tilo's and my mother's, mended a piece of what had broken apart at the Bishop's words.

"What will you do with him?" I asked, straightening and releasing the staff to her grasp.

She stepped back, blinking dew from her eyes. "He'll get what he deserves—groveling among those he's used in his game. You have only to listen to the melody of his song to know his fate." She winked and began to sing.

"There once was a man dressed all in white,
A greedy one was he.
Wandering from town to town was his plight,
Akin to no one was he.
He begged forgiveness with all his might,
A king among rats was he."

A sad smile creased my tear streaked cheeks, watching the two trot away into the misty night with the wind taking the lilting voice and scattering it amongst the hills and dells. I rubbed my eyes with the back of a hand and squatted down among the rats, shuddering with broken sobs. Wiglo came out of the lessening horde and scrambled up onto my shoulder. I lay back, turning my face to the moon until the tears stopped.

"Are you going to stay with me for what comes next?" I murmured, petting his soft fur with a forefinger sore from the long hours of playing.

I lay for a while there in the middle of the road trying to calm myself. The stones pressed into my back as I trembled and the pain felt good, centering. The rats began to disperse and with their leaving, I came back to myself bit by bit. Having played a human into doing my bidding had opened within me a part that was all Piper and felt not very much like Lucie.

"What would Tilo say?" I asked Wiglo where he sat cleaning his whiskers on my chest. "Perhaps he was right and this gift of song is double edged. I used to think that the question lay in, *can I do this thing;* when really it has always been, *what does it say about me if I go through with it.*"

Though my head was clearing, ice cold anger squeezed at my heart. I thought about my mother tied to the pyre in place of her sister. How she'd been held under torture and yet she had never declared herself to be Holda instead of Aythe. How abandoned she must have felt by her family, and the entire town.

"Aythe was right," I said, grimacing as I stood on stiff legs and picked up my flute case. "When you silence one of us, more will take up the song."

I took off toward town, foot sore and heart weary, and made it back to the red inn just before daybreak. My motley surcote was stained with the mud of the road and soot from climbing up and down walls all day so that it resembled less a pied minstrel outfit and more so a tattered and patched rag.

"It's late for you to be getting back," Agathe said from where she was busy kneading a row of bread boules.

I collapsed on the nearest bench, chin on the polished table pitted with knife marks.

"Woda," she called. "Bring some hot mead!"

"I'll be fine," I garbled. "Just need a moment."

Agathe eased me up as Woda put a warm mug to my lips. "Drink this and then we'll get you into bed. By the looks of you, you're due a good long rest."

I spluttered but managed to get some of the drink down.

"Finally did away with all those bells and your face paint, I see. But you're filthy." Woda scowled. "That mead has actually cleaned the bits of you it splashed down on."

"A bath, I think."

The two innkeepers nodded to each other in frank understanding and lifted me as if I were a babe into Woda's arms. I felt warm and safe, almost dozing against the woman's broad shoulders until gentle hands began to strip and wash me with a wet cloth.

"No," I breathed as they tsked over my soiled clothing and blistered feet. "I need that. Please don't cut it into rags."

"Rags? Burn it more like," Woda murmured.

"Need it? For what?" Agathe smiled down at me. "I heard your job was done here. There's talk that the streets were alive with vermin. And a pied minstrel leading them!"

I rubbed my eyes, heavy with sleep, to keep myself awake. "The Mayor," was all I could muster before falling into unconsciousness.

XI

The Piper

Dawn came and went and still I slept on. It wasn't until late afternoon that a soft whiskery prod in the ear woke me from my slumber. I snuffled awake.

"Wiglo?" I croaked, turning over. The rat climbed onto my chest and began cleaning an ear. "Is it time to go already?"

I rose, unsteady on my feet, and found that I had been laid to bed in a shift of rough homespun twice my size. The room was lit with a golden afternoon sunlight only seen in the early summer months and showed no sign of my motley anywhere. I crept out into the hall as silently as I could, Wiglo atop my shoulder as we peered over the railing into the common room below. A well-banked fire smoldered in the hearth at the far corner, but there was no sign of the two innkeepers nor any of the other guests.

"Hello?" I called down and still no one came out.

I tiptoed into the courtyard behind the inn where a line of clothes fluttered, drying in the breeze. Amongst the aprons and sheets flapped my almost unrecognizable motley doublet and stained hose. The rich dyes had all but faded after everything I'd put them through. The knees too had nothing but holes in them. I pulled them down.

"I can't see the Mayor in this," I whispered.

"You're the one they're calling the Piper, aren't you?"

I spun to see the drunk mercenary from my first night leaning in the doorway. She walked toward me, and I wrapped my arms around my overlarge shift, cautious without my motley costume to hide within.

"I'm Elze." She held out a hand

I took a step back. A knife glittered at her belt, and she was dressed in the traditional mercenary black.

"Sorry if I scared you," she said. "I just saw you running past my room in that nightgown. If you need them, you can borrow my spare set of clothes."

I squinted at her. "Why would you lend me your clothes?"

"You're an outsider here, as am I. People like us need to stick together."

"Like us?" I asked, my mind as thick as wool after too much sleep.

"I can see you don't trust me. And why should you?" She sighed. "Look, I came here to get my brother. I heard what happened a few months back—the witch trials. He's just an apprentice, but it's no longer safe here."

"And what makes you think it's not dangerous for you too? A foreign mercenary who stays at a red inn must stand out."

She set her hands on her hips and smiled. "It's only dangerous if you've got no one to watch your back. I saw you go off with the Mayor on feast day. He's not a man to trifle with."

I brushed the hair out of my eyes. "So you've been following me?"

"You made a bold entrance." Elze shrugged. "Look, I'm offering you help. Take it, or run off to meet with the most powerful man in the county in a borrowed shift. I'm sure he'll agree to whatever deal you have when he sees you're really nothing more than a slip of a country girl."

I frowned, wondering what Tilo or Aythe would have decided to do if they had been in my position. I rubbed my forehead. "All right, it's not like I have much of a choice," I said, thrusting out my chin.

"Good. I'll lay out my spare set of clothes before I leave." She glanced at my empty hands. "Where's your flute? Don't you always take it with you wherever you go?"

I looked down. I got a prickling sensation along my fingertips. Where was my flute? I hadn't seen it when I woke up now that I thought about it.

"Do you need it tonight?" she went on.

I shrugged, swallowing in a dry mouth. "It depends on whether the Mayor tries to break his word."

She looked at me, tilting her head. "Right, well good luck."

I waited for her to leave before I raced up to my room. I didn't have to go far, my flute case was on the windowsill next to the bed. I sank down slowly against the wall and let out a deep sigh. "Tonight, everything will be finished," I said. "If I play it right."

I took my time changing into her clothes. They were heavier than the soft surcote I was used to. The sun was just setting as I walked out the front doors of the red inn dressed in matching brown leathers and hose that smelled strongly of mead and another person's sweat. They fit me well enough. But up close, I knew it would look as if I were only playing at being a mercenary.

"That's why I'm doing this at night," I reminded myself, pushing a stray lock back from my eyes.

With my short hair combed back with a wet brush, I resembled a cocky youth, unproven but perhaps not to be messed with. I liked how I looked more than I'd thought I would, and I tried to ignore the confusion threatening to throw my struggling identity into even further chaos.

"I'm still the Piper," I whispered to myself and patted the flute case at my hip.

Groups of revelers crowded the streets as I made my way along the river. The whole town seemed to be out celebrating the end to the pestilence. None even glanced my way as I pushed through to stand across from the Mayor's manse. The lamps above the entry doors had been lit and candlesticks gleaming in each window. I leaned against a pillar across the street and took stock of the bustling small estate with all its guards coming and going. I waited until there was a lull and then slipped over the gate enclosing the back alley before shimmying up onto the terrace.

The Mayor was sitting facing me when I walked in. "Right on time," he said.

I hesitated between steps but smiled all the same. "Expecting me, were you?"

He looked me up and down. "Nice to see you don't always wear that ridiculous jester outfit." His eyes lingered on the flute case. "But still a minstrel at heart, I see."

I sketched a sardonic bow.

"Before we get down to business, I have one last question," the Mayor said. "Why here? Why not some other town?"

I grinned. "Let's just say I have a vested interest in those who hold to the old ways in this place."

"The witches?" he asked, brow knitting.

I grew still, the Piper within me itching to be heard. "Yes," I said. "And also with their children who've been made to bear up under the legacy of the Bishop's whims."

He eyed me closely. "Well it seems you took care of him."

"I did promise to remove *all* the town's vermin," I said, voice silky with delight. "Now that our bargain is at a close, tell me, is the writ ready?"

The Mayor sneered. "No."

"No?" I repeated, feeling the weight of his answer settle into my chest. I had never thought he would keep his promise willingly, but still it was hard to stomach what I'd have to do next.

The Mayor sneered. "Of course not. Why would you think a town such as ours would welcome whatever half-witted rabble who asks. We have our pride."

My mouth twisted as I felt that old thrill of vengeance take hold. "You sealed your word with blood. And that means you pay whether willingly or not."

His smile didn't reach his eyes. "Our deal was to get rid of the rats. And now I've found that the Bishop has disappeared too. Very worrisome indeed. Some are calling you a murderer, and I can't have a murder tied to me."

"Oh, King Rat, you mean? He's not dead." I didn't break my gaze as I said, "I thought you told me that if you found a single rat remaining, you'd break every one of my fingers. Isn't that right? I'm not responsible for the way the tune plays or who hears it."

The Mayor blinked at my nerve. "I should have you thrown into the oubliette for that."

"We both know I wouldn't go," I said. "At least not quietly." I patted the pocket that held the flute case, and he glanced between it and me.

"On your way then," he said, gesturing to the window. "Get as far as you can from here, and I won't have your tongue ripped out with hot pincers."

"What, and leave without payment?" I cocked my head. "You've gotten what you wanted, it would seem, and I'm not leaving until I get my side of the deal."

I reached in my pocket for my flute but found the case held a long thin dagger instead.

No flute.

I looked at the knife and my heart leapt into my mouth.

It was gone.

The air left my lungs.

The world grew dark at the edges.

I looked up and saw the Mayor was still talking, but I couldn't hear what he was saying over the rush of blood in my ears. For a paralyzing moment I gripped the dagger glinting in the halflight, thinking dark thoughts. But I was no killer. I learned that last night.

I tucked the knife into my belt loop next to where the now empty flute case dangled and leapt for the balcony. The Mayor didn't even stand as I swung over the railing. Escape was my only choice. I had failed, and now I had to run.

As soon as I landed on the cobblestone, rough hands grabbed me, shoving a cloth into my mouth so that I couldn't so much as hum a tune.

"Ah," the Mayor said from the balcony up above me. "And here I thought you were smarter than to leave the same way you'd come. You make this too easy."

I kicked and struggled but a sharp cuff had my head spinning.

I looked up, the world shifting around me as a figure to my right tossed up an object to the Mayor. It was long and slender and gleamed white in the moonlight. "Here's the flute, as promised."

I recognized that voice. "Elze," I murmured against the gag, trying to focus on the smug sneer across her face. I was about to curse her when I heard the sharp crack of bone breaking. Two pieces of flute fell to the cobbles at my feet. My eyes filled with tears, and I wanted to fall upon the broken remnants and mourn as if it were my mother's death all over again. But the two guards held me upright between them.

"No!"

I thought for a moment that it was my voice that had been torn unknowingly from my throat. But above me, behind the bulk of the Mayor, stood a slender girl in her night robe.

"Papa, no. That flute was magic," Gertrude said, her voice plaintive in the night. "It's a bad omen to destroy it."

"Hush, child." The Mayor rounded on his daughter, gesturing for a servant who took Gertrude in hand. "There'll be no more talk of magic in this house."

The servant dragged off the girl, and the Mayor turned back to me, a fair bit shakier than before.

"My appreciation for getting rid of the Bishop." He called down as one of his men held up a lamp to show my face. "He'd only been here for a season and already was making himself a nuisance. For that little service done, I'll have you killed quickly." The Mayor waved a hand lazily in our direction. "Show this piper what mercy looks like in our town."

The men shuffled me along, half dazed, to the quay where they threw me down and began to kick me. I covered my head and felt my stomach heave beneath my borrowed leather jerkin. I crawled away. A hard kick to my back pushed me over the lip of the causeway and down the stone steps. I landed in a groaning heap at the bottom. "Get the flute case," one said from the street above. Rough hands pulled out the case from my grasping fingers and crushed it beneath a poleaxe before kicking the pieces into the river.

"I'll finish it," one guard said and a boot kicked me over. "No need to waste more time on this runt. Not when there's mead flowing in every tavern." Just above the pounding of my heart and throbbing head, I heard jeers followed by their footsteps traveling back up and away from the river.

Blood filled my mouth around the gag, and I swallowed on reflex, choking on the warm salty wound of my own bitten tongue. I rolled my head back and coughed, blood and spittle speckling my face from my broken lips. To come so close and still to fail. The children would remain captives of whoever next proceeded the Bishop with none in the Gathering any the wiser. I had lost, after all. I could almost feel the river take my body, push it along its rocky underbelly to become food for fish and eels.

The guard crouched so close to me that I could hear the ragged breaths. "Won't you even look at me?" The guard's words held a smile.

I groaned and slitted open my eyes, fully expecting a sneer to be the last thing I saw.

Instead, Elze reached down and pulled out my gag.

"Why?" I breathed, confusion warring with betrayal as everything began to fall into place. How had the Mayor known to be ready tonight or what I'd look like out of my motley?

"I'm sorry, truly I am. But I knew they would kill you after what you did to the Bishop. And they needed to think they'd broken your magic flute."

"They did break my flute, didn't they?" I moaned, my thoughts muddled, and my head aching.

She shushed me and dragged me into the shadows of a grotto.

"I should never have trusted you." My hand twitched toward the dagger at my hip.

"Oh hush." She snatched it up, sheathing it on her belt. "I kicked you down the stairs to save you more of a beating. And besides, I didn't leave you empty handed. Not my fault if you didn't take your chances fighting."

"Why do you care?" I gurgled, swallowing a cough, and felt my ribs twinge. "Just leave me to die in peace."

She squinted. "Don't you see? Everyone gets what they want this way. The Mayor gets to save face among his men. I get paid off handsomely, and you..."

"I get thrown down a flight of stairs."

"You get to keep your flute." She laid the pipe on my heaving chest along with a bundle of motley.

My throat tightened, and I began to weep anew as I took my flute in my hands. I clutched it to my mouth and gave it a kiss with bloody lips right where the other two blood oath prints joined. It felt as if my spirit had been returned to me.

Elze sat back on her heels, watching me with a knowing smile. "It'll need some patches, but I trust it'll serve you for one more night." She took out a few coins and laid them alongside my flute. "This should at least cover your room and board."

"I don't want your blood money."

She gripped my hand so tightly it hurt and put the coins in my palm. "Have you forgotten how the world works? Gold will always get you farther than a kick to the head."

"No one could pay me enough to betray a trust." I spat blood into the dirt.

"Look, I learned long ago that the only way to get along in this world is to become the thing that men like the Mayor want you to be, and then use it against them."

"Become their monster," I spluttered. "Let them name me witch?"

"No," she said. "Piper...that's what they call you." Elze clenched her jaw. "And I may not have been completely straightforward with you earlier. I didn't learn about you just from my dealings with the Mayor. It was my brother who mentioned you to me."

"Brother?"

"Yes, you may not remember him. He works in the cathedral stables."

"Adelbert..." The memory came back to me of the easygoing groom from the stables. "He's your brother?"

"Yes." Elze stilled. "The guards took him in for questioning after the Bishop disappeared. Someone saw you talking to him."

I sat up straighter. "Is he okay?"

She glared at me. "He'll be fine now that I have the gold to pay his bail."

"I see." I slumped back with a hiss of pain.

"He told me it wasn't your fault and made me promise not to hurt you even if it meant his freedom. He always did have a soft heart."

I felt my lip tremble, and I clutched my flute tighter, looking down at it between my grubby fingers. "Brothers," I sighed. "What would we do without them?"

She gave me a sly grin. "They don't ever let you forget where you came from." With a departing pat on my flute, she stood and left.

The water lapped gently at my bare feet. I breathed slowly, feeling every cut and lump from my tumble down the stairs. I began to hum, a low soft melody, rich with purpose. When I heard the faint jingling of bells, I thought my ears must be ringing. It wasn't until Wiglo laid my jester's cap next to my face that I realized he must have sensed what I meant to do within my song. The pain and sorrow I'd felt just moments ago fell away, replaced with resolve.

"Perhaps there was only ever one way this deal was going to end." I held the motley before me, kneeling on the bank. I looked up and caught a glimpse of the old mill's rooftop beneath the moonlight in the distance.

XII

The Children

There, within the fog rolling off the banks of the river, a townswoman collected watercress in the grey light of dawn. She took her time to bend amongst the refuse, without the rats to crowd and nip at her ankles. The wind brought with it the promise of a bright, clear day. Lingering among the babbling river, an off-note raised the hairs along her arms, and the back of her neck. She shivered, and on shaking legs, the woman climbed the nearest quay stairs, peering over the edge and into the mist.

Along the streets, children moved as one, dancing in groups of twos and threes with the smallest carried along by their larger fellows.

They cavorted ever on with laughs and shouts and tapping steps, never tiring. But their eyes held the hollow grim of their ordeal, and of the shadow of long nights spent crying without solace. The street children who had remained just outside the Bishop's grasp, still covered in grime and skinny from the long winter, held hands and passed among them the bangled cap of the Piper, shaking it to and fro in glee. As the Piper neared, the woman ducked down, her eyes glued to the figure, shocked to see the silhouette of a young woman beneath the tattered motley surcote. The corners of the Piper's eyes creased with pain behind the smile of hard-won hope.

Townspeople crowded in their windows, watching the children dance toward the main gate. And in the lead played the Piper with bangled ankles jingling along to the song of a child's last night without a family. At the Piper's side danced a young girl, clad all in black with the remnant of a family crest embroidered on her cloak. The Mayor's young daughter, Gertrude. The villagers moved aside as the procession passed with a mixture of awe and penance, now that the Bishop no longer held sway. They only watched. It was as they'd always done, they were naught but magpies.

Murmurs rose around the townsfolk that the Mayor had tried to stop his daughter from joining the dance, but in the end he had been unable. It was said he'd been held back by what seemed to be hands no one could see, kept from moving toward his daughter, tears staining his eyes, crying out her name. And that the young girl was grinning as she danced down to meet the children, eager to be by the Piper's side. The Mayor had returned to his study thereafter, and, as if entranced, had pricked his wrist with a quill and put writ to his follies. The bloody note now hung nailed upon his front door for all to see and above it, the black figure of the Mayor stood on his balcony, watching the children leave.

Cloaked in shadows, figures moved among the black-trunked trees lining the road on the edge of the forest. When the procession reached the path leading to the southern glade, the Piper stopped, the tune falling apart to be carried off by the wind. People stepped out from behind the trees.

The children, no longer entranced, gasped and looked around, rosy cheeked and dazed in the sudden silence. A heartbeat of confusion was all it took before one called "Papa?" and then they were all running into the arms of those who loved them most. Even the rabble of orphans found cousins and neighbors who welcomed them gladly.

Lucie backed off the road until she came up against the peeling bark of a rowan tree. Tears streamed down her face in the sudden absence of the song, her mind trying to piece together all that had happened.

Gertrude squeezed her hand, looking up with wet eyes. "You're so brave."

Lucie knelt and pulled the girl into a tight hug.

Tilo pushed through the crowd to his sister, his grin faltering as he came closer.

"Hello, brother." She released Gertrude and took a moment to return to herself, still so full of the lilting children's music pulsing within her. She tried to get her voice to work again, to sound like she used to when she was just his sister, but it was not easy.

"I'm glad you came back to us!"

"It was a near thing." She swallowed and felt a loose tooth shift beneath her tongue.

He glanced down at the bloody flute and then back up to her bruised face. His smile faltered. "Where's Aythe?"

"Gone. She got what she came for." Lucie reluctantly slipped her mother's flute back into a pocket, recalling the moment when she'd learned what kind of person their aunt truly was.

"We'll be safe now," Tilo said with such conviction that Lucie laughed. It broke from her, harsh and bitter.

"Where will we go?" Gertrude asked, shielding her eyes with a hand as she looked around at the reunions.

"I've been thinking on that." Tilo pointed off into the distant forest. "We'll make a town of our own," he said. "No one will ever need to wander in search of a home again."

Lucie smiled bitter and closed-mouthed; her brother still understood nothing of what had happened or why those men had done what they did. Her fists clenched until her knuckles whitened. She shook her head, a strong urge to take her flute back out and return to town gripped her so that she had to close her eyes against it. She did not want to be like Aythe.

"What more can we do, Lucie?" he asked. It was the tone he'd always used to take her down a notch.

She wanted to scream, but she had learned that there was a better way. She lowered her voice so that it held the coaxing edge of the Piper's tone. "The people that caused this won't stop, Tilo. Unless someone forces them to."

Gertrude took a step back, and Tilo glanced at the crowd behind him, but it seemed no one had heard. He turned back to Lucie, his hands stretched out but didn't move closer.

"Lucie, I never wanted this for you. This is Aythe's way."

The words quenched her anger, but left her cold. "If you knew what happened...what I had to do, you—" her voice broke, and she took a breath to steady herself. "I am not Aythe. But I'm also not afraid to do what must be done."

Tilo's voice was soft as he said, "I can see that this has cost you. We both know you were the only one who could have done it." He turned to the Gathering behind him, and she followed his gaze. "I want more for them than what we had," he said. "These children deserve a fresh start, a home that isn't tinged with the memory of what we've overcome." He turned back to her. "No more lies, no more vengeance."

She looked between Gertrude's large-eyed stare and Tilo's open expression. No matter what he said, he would never know exactly what it had cost her. She still wasn't sure herself, but a dark promise lingered within her chest. It abided.

"Okay," she said, straightening her surcote. "Let's build something new, for everyone."

Tilo smiled.

Gertrude hugged her.

Scratching broke from the brush at her feet and Wiglo ran up the trunk to sit on a dead branch. His small eyes watched her as he cleaned his whiskers of blood. Something stirred within her chest and the Piper ran her thumb along the bloody tip of the flute. She'd have to carve a new case. It would be slim and lightweight, but strong...and with her, always.

Acknowledgments

The first people I owe thanks to are my fellow writers who have inspired and supported me, handling every critique draft as if it were their own over the years. Writers are irreplaceable friends and I've been lucky enough to work with some fantastic ones. In particular, Nicole, who coerced me, not so gently, to get back into writing after a decade-long hiatus. I think about our conversations on the veranda every time I want to give up on a story. Also, to the local writers' group, namely Meg, Shaun and Vince for lending their knowledge and support. And to my online writing community in Clarion West with a special thanks to Hannya, Parker, AEN Russell, Baxter, and Jenifer.

This novella began as a flash piece that I wrote in the final week of a flash fiction critique group. The prompt was something like "fairytale retellings" and it felt far outside my comfort zone. I typically write science fiction with a futuristic feel even though historical fiction is my favorite genre to read. What made it onto the page surprised me. It was a story of hardship and music and change. I've always been fascinated by the speculations around the Pied Piper—

were the children carried off by typhus? Taken as oblates for a crusade? I thought of the person who could lead an entire town's worth of children away with a song at dawn. And, thus, the Piper came to life.

A lot of research went into the world surrounding our piper. The Museum Hameln has a fantastic compilation of all the Pied Piper speculations and works along with a rich history of the town itself. The city of Strasbourg in Alsace also has my thanks as a semester studying there informed the creation of the town across the river, particularly the single-spire cathedral. The historical fantasy books that showed me how strong women could be in this genre include Nicola Griffith's *Spear* and *Hild*, *The Bear and the Nightingale* by Katherine Arden, and *Nettle and Bone* by T. Kingfisher. These are only a few of the many that have sucked me in and stuck with me.

My local public library and its affiliates played an integral part in the historical research. Notable works include: Benjamin Arnold's *Count and Bishop in Medieval Germany: A Study of Regional Power, 1100-1350* and "German Bishops and their Military Retinues in the Medieval Empire" in Volume 7, Issue 2 of *German History*; "The Liturgical Role of Children in Monastic Customaries from the Central Middle Ages" by Susan Boynton; *Scribes for Women's Convents in Late Medieval Germany* by Cynthia J. Cyrus; *Schools and Schooling in Late Medieval Germany: Regensbur, 1250-1500* by David Sheffler; *The Germanization of Early Medieval Christianity: A Sociohistorical Approach to Religious Transformation* by James C. Russell; *Oblation or Obligation? A Canonical Ambiguity* by John Doran; *The Sacred & the Sinister: Studies in Medieval Religion and Magic* edited by David J. Collins, S.J.; *The Rise of Magic in Early Medieval Europe* by Valerie I. J. Flint; *Feminine Figurae: Representations of Gender in Religious Texts by Medieval German Women Writers 1100-1375* by Rebecca L. R. Garber; *Rules and Rituals in Medieval Power Games* by Gerd Althoff; and *Conflicting Femininities in Medieval German Literature* by Karina Marie Ash.

Also, thank you to everyone who helped bring *Pay the Piper* to life: Artist Aleeya Jones for the gorgeous cover, Speculation Publications' LC Allingham and River Eno for your incredible talent and guidance. Your belief in this story and in myself has meant the world.

And finally, a big thank you to everyone who found their way to our Kickstarter page and supported this project. Because of your contribution, *Pay the Piper* is now a fully fledged work of art. You are all most appreciated: Jason Ryder, Ferra Bear and Ivy Bum MacGillivray, Mike Petty, Amanda Tegtmeyer, Vince Vasudevan, Josh Jackson, Kian and Stacey Sangtian, William Millar, Julia Chiarelli, Chase McGlinchey, Edward Abbott, Sean Bear, Graham Huffman, Victoria P, Ef Deal, Kathy Puleio, Ann Stolinsky, Lyss, Michelle Wire, Sergey Kochergan, Jackie MacVean, Sarah Houghton, William J. Donahue, Dave Ring, Megan Fencil, David K Mitchell, Simon K, Susan Tulio, Martha Connell, Olga Yolgina, Allison Thurman, Lyss, T Connell, Victoria Green, Kevin Connell and Coco DeNucci.

About the Author

Sarah Connell is the author of the science-fiction trilogy Project Awakening. Her short stories have appeared in magazines and anthologies around the world. Her writing evokes the places where she's lived and worked, from ranches on the outskirts of Yellowstone to the southern gothic cityscape of Charleston. Growing up, some of her earliest memories are sitting by the wood stove in her grandfather's studio, surrounded by the smell of oil paint and canvas. She began to write while studying in Strasbourg, France. The city on the edge of Alsace lends itself to storytelling with winding streets of centuries-old tanner houses leading to the medieval cathedral. Her experiences there are the seed for Pay the Piper. She currently lives in the Carolinas with her person and their cat, Lyra.

Other books by Sarah Connell:
The Project Awakening Series:

The Inventors

The Awards

The Awakening

sarah-connell.com

Check out the Collections of Utter Speculation
The Lost Colony of Roanoke
The Jersey Devil
Lady in White
The Dancing Plague
Cry Baby Bridge
Novellas of Utter Speculation:
Pay the Piper by Sarah Connell
New Title TBA Summer 2025

And our other Books
Incubate: a horror collection of feminine power
Work in Progress: Story Crafting Notebook
Beach Shorts
Yule
Evergreen
Muse
Grimm Retold
Vampire Hunters: An Incomplete Record of Personal Accounts

www.speculationpub.com